Does Lightning Strike Twice?

REGINA PRICE

authorHOUSE®

AuthorHouse™
1663 Liberty Drive
Bloomington, IN 47403
www.authorhouse.com
Phone: 1 (800) 839-8640

This is a work of fiction. All of the characters, names, incidents, organizations, and dialogue in this novel are either the products of the author's imagination or are used fictitiously.

Published by AuthorHouse 06/27/2019

ISBN: 978-1-7283-1753-3 (sc)
ISBN: 978-1-7283-1752-6 (hc)
ISBN: 978-1-7283-1754-0 (e)

Library of Congress Control Number: 2019908711

Print information available on the last page.

Chapter One

Prison is the answer, I decide.

Most people would view the spectacle of a wife and mother entering state prison as a tragedy. I see it as a way of gaining family harmony as well as great wealth and fame.

I think about this while chipping ice off the windshield of our snowy beige Mark III Chevy conversion van. It's another dreary Maine morning. But what do you expect when you live in a part of the country that is north of most of the populated areas of Canada?

I've been working on the ice for twenty minutes when my friend and next-door neighbor Barb breaks my reverie. "Happy Birthday, Molly." Barb talks to me from her cocoa-colored Mercedes station wagon. I suspect it's all nice and warm because her husband Mitchell went out early to start it for her. Inside the Mercedes is her one perfect child, Billy, who I think will one day marry Chelsea Clinton's best friend.

Barb puts her warm luxury vehicle into park and gets out. She looks great. She always looks great but Barb has a little something beyond that. It's what makes her Barb. The best way I can explain it is to tell you that Barb wears her mink everywhere. Not just to the opera or out to dinner. Barb wears it to Shoppers Fair, to the pharmacy, to school conferences, even to the ice rink. She knows that this is politically incorrect and she doesn't care. This is one of the reasons I love her.

She frowns. "You'll never get that windshield done in time. You're riding with me."

I shake my head. "We'll never fit in your car." After all, I do have four hockey-playing sons to her one. This is the one and probably only area where I have outdone my friend: the human being production department.

Barb raises her left eyebrow a fraction of an inch. "So? Somebody can ride on top."

Although I admire her bravado, I still cannot stop the fear that sweeps over me as I view the reaction of my four darlings, sweet sons of my youth. Standing together in the garage in full hockey equipment, Dash Junior, Bobby, Wayne (named after the Great Gretsky), and Dart, fully dressed in shoulder pads, neck guards, elbow guards, shin guards, and hockey pants are a formidable sight. I wonder, what if they get mad and hit me with their hockey sticks? But I get a grip. After all, this is my family.

Fifteen-year-old Junior begins. "The wagon? We'll never fit in the wagon, not with all this equipment." Junior's lower lip goes out. He's the most like me and I recognize this sure sign of trouble. "Has Dad left yet?"

I wonder how he can even ask this question since everyday our morning routine is exactly the same. First Dash leaves to visit his construction site. Then I drive the boys to the rink. Then Dash drives to the rink to coach the boys' teams. "We'll put the hockey bags on top," I respond calmly.

Bobby, my second son, whose main claim to fame (besides the fact that he is named after hockey legend, Bobby Orr) is that he is the fastest skater in the family and has the best left to right fake, decides to help his older brother. "Dad said never to do that. Dad says the road dirt can ruin the equipment. What's wrong with the van?"

I have learned a few things about handling my brood and one of them is not to explain. Explanations are immediately seen as indices of weakness. So I look sternly at all four. "Put the bags on top of Mrs. Richmond's car."

Bobby, who I know is destined to be a lawyer someday, pulls himself up to his full height. "Mom, I just want you to know that if there's any problem here like missing screws on the helmet, misalignment of the cage, torn straps, I'm going to have to tell Dad."

"Thanks for the warning," I am only half-sarcastic because I know that Bobby truly believes he is doing me a favor by expressing his displeasure directly to me. This, he figures, gives me a chance to correct my misbehavior before he has to take it up directly with his father, my husband, the coach; so my fledgling F. Lee Bailey does have a soft spot in his heart for me.

As Barb and I make our daily pilgrimage to the ice rink for one of the various practices that have been scheduled for every damn day of the week, we say little, because the population of the car is really broken into camps: them and us. It's a little like a car ride with Al Sharpton and Rush Limbaugh. What is there to say that won't result in a physical confrontation? Barb makes just one comment. She knows it's safe because the boys won't understand it. "Did you have that dream again last night?"

I nod my head. I've been having a recurring dream that runs like a reel of film, always the same, frame by frame, except that each time it plays, it goes just a little bit farther. This dream is absolutely the sweetest most pleasurable nighttime thing that's happened to me in years. And yes, that includes sex and Hagen-Daaz at midnight.

"I like that dream." Barb shoots me a conspiratorial glance, which holds us until we get to the rink and our miserable sulky sons hurry off to the arena except for Billy, the one perfect child, who hangs back to say goodbye to his mother. After he leaves, when we are alone in the car at last, I relate to Barb the delicious details of the dream.

The dream always begins the same way. It's your standard Hollywood party. Working the door is private security in silk shirts and Nikes. Inside it's glitz and lox. It's a small gathering, really. Just Demi and her group, and Nicholson and his group, and Cruise, of course Cruise.

Although I live my life running the forgotten sneakers to school and keeping the laundry white and bright, although I have never even been to L.A., let alone a Hollywood party, all this feels perfectly natural and comfy.

Anyway, <u>he</u> comes in. The crowd parts. He wears casual California clothes but nothing gaudy. He isn't physically large yet he gives the appearance of being massive. At all times he is the essence of mogul. He is, after all... Sylvester Stallone (actually he is the young Sylvester Stallone looking as he did in his first Rocky movie.)

Now, I know Stallone sprays the room with bullets. I know he did his action hero sequels into the ground. I know he's not exactly a hero of the literati. But believe me <u>I</u> have not been inviting him into my bedroom every night. He's just coming.

There is a bright, intense quality to the light around Sylvester, but I disregard it and settle down to the obvious fact that Sylvester is drawn to

3

me. I should mention at this point that I am modestly dressed, not in the dirty snow boots that I use for most of the Maine winters, but in a dark green velvet dress that for some reason makes all the six foot blondes look pale or ill, as if they've eaten too many oysters and maybe will vomit.

While Sylvester is captivated by my beauty (the power of which is recognized by every man and woman in the room and this is one of the very best parts of the dream) there is something else about me that mesmerizes Sylvester. Across the crowded room, he walks to me.

He looks down at me with heavy lidded eyes and says, "Adrian, would you take off your hat?" Up until this time I did not know my name was Adrian. But I smile, I like it. Sylvester has such an amazing voice, nothing like that brutish slur he uses in the movies. No, this is a deep, masculine, intellectual voice. For some reason it rouses in me an animal response and I feel I have to make a meaningful reply. Since I wear no hat, I take off my hair instead.

No matter, Sylvester likes me just as well bald.

As we talk, I have his rapt attention. With my naive provincial Northeastern attitudes, I have captured him. I am something exotic to Southern California. I am genuine...I am the real thing.

He remains at my side for the entire evening, completely ignoring his gorgeous blond companions. We don't drink. We don't party. We just stare into each other's eyes.

As the evening progresses and I become more aware of the real Stallone, his drive, his successes, the problems of creative overexposure, the art forgery, I realize that he is nothing like his Hollywood image. He is smart. He is funny. And he has an encyclopedic knowledge of the history of Ancient Rome. But as we chat I also realize that woven like a thread through everything we discuss is our overriding interest and appreciation of story and this is really what draws us together. Even though it seems to be a powerful, vibrant, even sexual force, it is really the meeting of two minds, the fusion of two souls. We both love stories.

Incidentally I try not to flirt, but I am so good at it, I just can't help myself. Naturally he is charmed. Sylvester, being a man, doesn't immediately understand our true destiny. Totally smitten and completely in love, he makes a play for me. Still he retains the dignity befitting a great figure of contemporary entertainment, Hollywood hero, and mogul.

Meaning he does not get down on his knees. (This is another really good part.)

I am able to turn him down not because I can resist those heavy lidded eyes or those sinewy pectorals, biceps, and triceps but because I, in my woman's fashion, have already realized what the true nature of our relationship will be. I take a deep breath.

Chapter Two

I turn to Barb. "And that is where the dream ends."

Barb lets out a loud groan. "You screwed up the ending. The right ending is when he gets down on his knees, you make a prenuptial agreement, and become Mrs. Sylvester Stallone."

"No, no," I protest. "He proposed marriage and even waived the prenupt."

"You failed to mention that." Barb slips a Tic-Tac between her teeth. "So?"

"It just didn't feel right."

Barb is grumpy now. She doesn't understand. I try to explain to her that Sylvester requires two psychiatrists to help him overcome his severe depression due to my rejection of his marriage proposal, but Barb doesn't care. She's disgusted with me. Barb feels that the true test in the world of female life, is: Are you good at being a woman?

Sometimes I wonder if she isn't right about that. We head into the ice rink to watch the first practice, which is actually for Dart and Billy Richmond's team.

In the winter, when you go into a building, you expect to find warmth. After all it is a human-built place of comfort and relief against the elements. Not so our ice rink. Built of stone fifty years ago for the purpose of providing space for the showing of thoroughbred horses, our ice arena is actually colder inside than outside. The stone holds the cold, and the ice-making equipment adds a bitter chill. So what you feel when you walk into our ice rink during the winter is actually a blast of cold air.

There is also a particular sound that a parent eventually grows to love or hate. It is the sound of the skates on the playing surface - the sound of steel on ice. And this sound blends with a cold indescribable smell...the smell of the ice.

As Barb and I walk, we see huddled around the curved boards of the rink, the mothers of hockey. Like the baba of the Ukraine (I am currently studying Russian and drama), they are noisy boisterous matrons. Their derrieres are enormous globules of fat, pressed sausage-like into tight blue jeans, and as they line up against the side of the rink, they appear to be chubby links in the same sausage.

Whenever Barb sees them, she hisses like a vampire who has seen a cross. "Widebodies," she says disdainfully. I myself say nothing because I am forty pounds overweight and while I do not wear jeans, I am too close to their poundage to make any judgments.

Actually I have noticed that most of the women in this arena are fat, or at least chubby. In fact Barb is the only thin woman in the building. When I asked her one day why this was, she answered, "Simple, I'm a bitch and bitches never get fat."

Barb and I move over to the sideboards where the rest of the parents are watching. Some parents just love to watch but I have never felt that way. Usually I while away my time with coffee and glazed doughnuts from the snack bar. Barb never eats anything from the snack bar. She doesn't even drink the coffee. She says the coffee is too close to the doughnuts.

As the two teams scrimmage, one twelve-year-old spears another. In hockey (a/k/a the H word) spearing means that your opponent butt-ends the hockey stick into your body, preferably into your solar plexus, the one place your padding may not reach. I know this because I have seen it happen to my sons. I have also seen my sons expertly execute this manuever on others. As the injured player lies on the ice, Barb's husband Mitchell Richmond slides across the ice in his L.L. Bean snow sneakers to see how the boy is.

My husband Dash, the team coach, skates over to Barb and me, executing a one-footed speed stop that would have sprayed us with snow were it not for the boards between us. "They're tough today," he says proudly.

Lately when I look at him, it's as if I'd never seen him before. He is a big, good-looking man. I used to think he had intelligent eyes. In fact, I used to think he was an intellectual. After all we took journalism together

7

in college, and Dash did work as a sports reporter for the <u>Bangor Gazette</u> before he took over the family construction business. And he still teaches journalism part-time at the university, which is why he has been so tolerant of my constant course-taking. (I have three post-graduate degrees, and all the credits were free.)

My eyes travel from Mitchell tending the downed player, back to Dash. Mitchell looks his forty years because his hair has thinned a bit, his waistline thickened. Dash, except for a few facial lines, is as hard and lean as when we first met.

And I now know why - because Dash is a jock. I don't know how that fact eluded me for so long. I guess it's a question of primary orientation. Yes, Dash is a business man and yes, he is a teacher, but first and foremost he is a jock. I sigh unconsciously. I hate jocks and I have no idea how I ended up married to one.

The injured boy still has not gotten up, meaning that soon Dash will have to make a show of perfunctory concern by skating over there. I raise my arm thinking I will touch Dash who's only inches away. Instead I do the craziest thing. I actually make a request.

"Let's go out for dinner tonight. I have a sitter and it's my birthday." I don't point out that he seems to have forgotten this birthday which is my Big Four-oh, just as he has forgotten the previous two others.

Dash looks at me as if I have lost contact with reality. "There's a game tonight."

"There's a game every night."

But the injured boy is up and Dash skates away, happy to have escaped without having to answer. I watch him as he glides confidently over the frozen surface and Barb remarks, "He's in great shape, isn't he?" Perception, I think, is all a matter of distance.

With practiced ease I shake off Dash's rejection. One more doughnut and coffee later, we are all repacked like sardines in Barb's car, on the round trip taking the boys to school. And I know that after this, I can relax and talk to Gita.

My therapist, Gita Habandouge and I meet once a week, which usually works out well for both of us. But this has been an especially hard week for me and my feelings are pent-up to the point that I feel close to bursting. With every atom in my being, I yearn to tell her exactly what I need to do.

Chapter Three

"I want to reach right into his chest with my bare hands, in a style similar to that of the ancient Mayan priests and pull his still beating heart from his chest."

Gita, merely hmms me.

"I want to hang him by his hands and slowly lower him into a pit of ravenous jackals." This is an actual punishment from the deterioration of the Roman empire around the time of the reign of Galba.

This merits only a nod.

"I want to stop cooking...forever."

This time my psychiatrist, Gita Haboudange looks up. She has bleached blond permed hair and red glasses like Sally Jesse Raphael. Gita stretches her spine and looks at me. She even pulls off the red glasses, a gesture she reserves for the most serious situations. "That's a good expression of your feelings. But you do realize that is exactly what you said last week?"

"No," I protest. I'm sure she is mistaken. I have only been coming to this beautiful little safe house for two and a half years. I have only begun to delineate my problem. I cannot have repeated myself.

"Would you like me to play back last week's tape?"

I look down at the still running tape recorder. I should never have allowed her to tape me in the first place. But then who would have thought that a member of the healing profession would use it for such cruel purpose?

Gita stands authoritatively. All winter she wears only the brightest colors: aluminium jackets, wild print pants, red purses, pink shoes. And she wears them all together. Today she wears a fuchsia cashmere sweater, black stretch pants, and silver shoes. My theory is that the only reason

Gita can make these clothing choices and still have a practice is that she is trained in Freudian and Jungian analysis as well as behavior modification and neuro-linguistic programming. As always her movements are full of strength and intensity, just like her deep heavily accented voice. "Molly, what have you learned in the past two years?"

I shrug.

"Molly, I want you to look at the photographs on my wall."

I am surprised that I have never noticed these gold-framed photographs before; I am sure she must have just put them up. After all, I have memorized this room, from the mahogany wainscotting to the burgundy velvet draperies. Everywhere there are statues of women: a Chinese geisha, Joan of Arc, Amazonian warriors. Inside this office I have always felt safe and protected. But now Gita has opened her mouth to speak, and as always I am verbally overwhelmed by her. "This is Mahtob. This is Maryam. This is my mother and this is me."

I study the photographs, which all depict women in black chadors photographed in brilliant sunlight against bleached stone walls. They all look like shadows. "You don't look like yourself," I answer, squinting to figure out which one of the black shadows is Gita.

But now Gita draws me away from the pictures with her intense voice and fixes me with her sunken eyes. "This is how I grew up in Iran. Veiled. Rules about what I could eat, when I could eat, what I could say, who I could talk to. More rules than you can imagine. But look at me now, I am a different woman."

This helps me understand why Gita wears all the colors of the rainbow at the same time. She's just making up for lost time. Again she draws me in with her mesmerizing foreign voice. "But I did not become the woman I am today by standard therapy. You know what standard therapy is. That's what we we've been doing together. You come in and tell me your feelings and I respond, and we wait for you to come to new ideas. It's okay, but it's so wasteful of time."

Immediately I get nervous. She's not going to cut me off, is she? Just when I've gotten used to coming here, just when I trust her enough to get down and really complain, really bitch. She wouldn't do that to me, would she? I look at her with real fear. "But, Gita, I feel so much better after coming in here." For emphasis I touch her hand.

"Sure," she says brusquely, almost unfeelingly. "But what about change? Has anything really changed for you since you've been coming here?"

Quickly I review what I know about therapy relationships. It's my understanding that the shrinkor is supposed to let the shrinkee come to her own personal revelations at her own personal pace. But what can I do? I can't exactly threaten to sue her without disturbing our therapeutic relationship.

Gita waves her red glasses at me. "You still have your headaches," she accuses me.

I nod guiltily, but I'm also thinking. Is there a timetable here? Have I failed a test? Am I on some kind of schedule that nobody told me about? My basic plan was to come in here weekly and unload my complaints. Meanwhile, I would continue to live with my demanding, difficult husband. It seemed to me to be a superior plan devised by a bright and unusually creative mind.

"And your weight, you told me you're still overeating. You know what they say about food, Molly?"

"No," I say dully.

"Food is Love."

This makes me so uncomfortable that I try to distract her. "I had that dream again, the one about Sylvester Stallone. I'm having it every night now."

"Molly, listen to me." Uh-oh. I can tell from that really deep timbre in her voice that distracting her isn't going to work. "Molly, I want to do a new therapy with you. I want you to go home tonight and confront your husband."

"Confront my husband? How can I confront someone who ignores me?"

"But you are a woman who cannot be ignored," Gita tells me in that deep, mesmerizing voice.

"I am?"

"Yes and this time when you tell your husband the way you feel and he changes the subject or walks away from you, you will stay 'In his face'. That's what I call this new treatment, 'In his face'."

Gita fixes me with her magnificent Middle Eastern eyes. "Do this, Molly. This will work." I would like it to work, I think slowly, I would like something to work.

"Don't get emotional and don't fight. Lift yourself above the dispute but stay 'In his face' until he answers your questions."

"Questions?" I wonder out loud. "What am I supposed to ask him?"

"Whatever you want."

"I just don't understand the motivation for my insisting that Dash answer questions," I say in an effort to slow Gita down because I don't want to get pressured into making any performance promises here. If I do, I know that next week Gita will expect me to tell her what happened and then I will have to make something up. I realize that lying to one's therapist is not very cost-effective but sometimes, it's just the easiest thing.

"You are searching for the truth, Molly."

"It sounds very," I struggle for the right word, "aggravating."

"Therapy isn't about feeling good, Molly. Therapy is about knowledge." Gita pauses here for effect. "And, Molly, knowledge is power."

"I've never been into power," I say, squirming in the burgundy leather recliner.

Gita licks her lips. "How about freedom?"

The word rolls around in my head for a moment like a childhood memory. Freedom - it smells like fresh breezes and walks by the sea, it sounds like the rattling of palm trees in the morning wind, and I am forced to admit, "Freedom is definitely a desirable concept."

Naturally Gita presses her advantage. "So you agree to try this?"

Chapter Four

As I drive my Chevy van down snowy Genesee Street, I push up my glasses and massage the bridge of my nose knowing full well I shouldn't have agreed to Gita's demands. I told her last week that today was my birthday just like I told her that this morning I was scheduled for the big meeting with my literary group. Obviously I have enough on my mind. She shouldn't have pressed me. Gita's been getting entirely too pushy lately.

As I'm driving along in my van I look down at the drivers of the other cars. They always give me plenty of room when I'm driving this thing. I think they're afraid of me. Even if buying it was Dash's idea, even if the major purpose of the van is to transport us to the H word activities: hockey games, hotels, AHA conferences, coaching seminars, referee courses, I still love it.

For one thing, it's like a little house on wheels. You can read in it, sleep in it, eat, watch t.v., or play Nintendo. What sane working parent wouldn't pay an extra $1,400 for a vehicle option guaranteed to totally anesthetize the entire family for the duration of any trip?

But my love for this van goes deeper than that. The reason I'm so crazy about Victor (Naming the van was an irristible impulse) is that when I'm driving down the highway, eye-to-eye with the truckers, I experience a feeling that I haven't felt in a long time.

I feel strong and powerful. Of course my usual wimpiness may have something to do with my life choices. The fact that I've been writing fiction in my basement for years and without making a single sale, hasn't done much for my self-esteem.

I have to admit I never expected to have such a long apprenticeship in the writing world. Because at the age of nine I began my first novel which was about a girl named Molly who - surprise, surprise- was actually me. Molly controlled everything in the world. The mechanics of domination were such that the world and its inhabitants had free will until something happened that I didn't like. That night I would decide what necessary changes would be made to rectify the injustice of the day. My unlimited power was a secret. No one knew or would ever know or find out that I was really the ruler of the universe.

In other words, in the fourth grade, you might get away with calling me a geekoid at recess on Tuesday. But I can guarantee that by Wednesday morning a second nose would be growing on your face.

I felt then as I do now that this healthy desire for justice is the motivating drive behind my writing. What I don't understand is why it's taking so long for my talent to be recognized when I have always known in my bones, in my gut, in all those places where you get the really true feelings (and this eliminates the head) that I would be a great writer.

Let me define great - Great as in perceptive, wise, incisive, mythical, even astounding but always an author who delivers a fast, compelling read. So I was stunned when my first effort was rejected. It was my suspense thriller about a murderous district attorney who is also an aerobics instructor and speech pathologist. I figured I already had the law degree (one of my three post graduate degrees) and I have taken a few aerobics classes, so I was a natural to develop a blockbuster in this particular genre.

When this did not occur, I bounced back by enrolling in the university's Creative Writing Program. During this intense period, I learned that Ernest Hemingway is the king or "Papa" of the minimalist school of literary writing. I also learned that even though Ernest said, "Good writers compete only with the dead" there are lots of living minimalists writing in this spare modern style.

During this two year program culminating in a Master of Arts Degree, I wrote a collection of short stories about middle class, middle aged housewives doing things like cooking and gardening. But you know this style of writing is really pared down. They don't want you using unnecessary words, unnecessary characters and most of all they don't want your characters embarking on unnecessary or unbelievable actions. I have trouble writing like that, maybe it's because I'm really not a minimalist person.

So all the while I'm writing my short stories, I have to give vent to my real personality by writing something lively...something fun. Soon I have over four hundred pages of a detective novel. The working title is <u>Margaret White, P.I.</u> Margaret is a free thinking gal of indeterminate age, a private investigator who has her own unique style.

Today my writing group has agreed to depart from their usual format (ordinarily we draw numbers to determine the reading order and offer criticism round-robin as each reader finishes) and will spend the full time critiquing my novel, copies of which I distributed last week.

So it is with great anticipation that I park my big beige Chevy house on wheels in front of the home of Rachel Durrell who has always hosted our meetings. I make my way up the walk and pass through those big doors with the artistic leaded spiderweb windows. Apropos, I think, for the years I have spent coming to the house.

The front hall of Rachel's house is conspicuously adorned with Mapplethorpe photos: <u>The Calla Lilly, 1987</u>, <u>The Eggplant, 1985</u>. There are also a few prints by David Hockney and Roy Lichtenstein. In Rachel's den, the bookcases are full of the favorite thinking books of the nineties: Susan Faludi, Germaine Greer, a treatise on South Africa, not to mention the latest novella by the new Japanese author about a teenage transsexual. I sigh, everything nowadays seems to be about transsexuality.

Today Rachel is wearing her favorite "The Devil loves me" t-shirt, which she stole from her daughter Sasha, who is a vegetarian Satanist and who despite her razor haircut is still a dead ringer for Margaret Hamilton as the Wicked Witch of the West. In the writing group whenever Rachel mentions anything about Sasha, everyone chuckles indulgently at Sasha's stages. These stages involve picking up strangers on the street whom her mother cheerfully boards, cutting school when there is no protest to organize, and disappearing for long weekends to convene with her coven.

My personal opinion is that if I opened the morning paper to learn that Rachel had been disemboweled and eaten by Sasha and her friends I would be surprised only that Sasha had broken her vows to the Great God "Vegetable." But hey, I've got my own problems at home.

I am a little late and have missed the chatting time. My group is mostly published authors, all graduates of the university's writing program, and even if I never did really fit with the program, I still am eager to hear what they have to say. Most especially I want to hear the opinion of Gordon Durkee.

Gordon is the only person in the group who has published a full length novel. Actually he has published several well reviewed novels and has received a nomination for the PEN/Faulkner Award. He has just returned from a two-year sabbatical in New York City, time well spent socializing with the literati of the Upper West Side. Despite his success, I have always considered Gordon a friend as well as a colleague. So I'm really optimistic right up until the moment when Gordon turns his squinty little eyes on me and declares. "Penis envy."

Chapter Five

"Penis envy?" I stammer.

Gordon is the unofficial leader of our writing group and there is no close second whom I can turn to for help. Even though I was able to parlay my M.A. in creative writing into a part time job teaching fiction at Carlson Community College, that counts for nothing around here because Gordon's star has eclipsed us all. He actually has literary friends who call him from not just New York but also London, Paris, and Marbella. Several responses pass through my mind but Gordon is literally just too big to insult. Feigning my best Miss Piggy pose, I try "Penis envy? Moi?" This is probably a little too cute, but it goes over, everybody laughs, and I am off the hook. Not that I am afraid of Gordon. I can write just as well as Gordon. No, I can probably write better than Gordon. But Gordon is a success and I am not.

Sometimes I wonder if my traditionalism has something to do with it. I'm really not a nineties kind of woman. I think I'm actually a seventies kind of woman or maybe a fifties kind of woman. Let's face it, I'm really retro.

To begin with I'm straight. I know, it's hard to believe. I'm a woman whose sexual fantasies are all about men. I don't think it would be fun to fool around with a woman just for the heck of it. I don't want to be tied up and I don't want to pose naked on the Miami freeway.

Another thing that puts me several years behind modern is the fact that I seem to be locked into this wife and mother thing which as everyone knows is hopelessly retro. Okay, now I have alienated everyone. And right now I'm afraid I'm going to have to pay. I fear Gordon's little remark about penis envy was just a riposte. I prepare myself for the full lunge.

"Why is your main character -what's her name?- Margaret White..." Gordon sneers a little at the name because it registers no ethnicity on his P.C. scale, "Why is this character interested in this crime? Not only interested but by this second chapter she is actually involved in solving this crime?" Another sneer.

"Gordon, they killed her sister."

"Of course, but the police can take care of that sort of thing." Gordon seems to think we live in pre-World War II Germany and the police are incredibly efficient. But since Gordon is the leader, everyone nods robotically. After all, hasn't he successfully directed us through the temptations of frivolous work, past the miasmic swamp of commerciality to the high shore of modern psychological and political correctness? And now Gordon with great authority is going for the red meat. "And why does your heroine have a gun?"

At this, all nod in fervent agreement. A few voices add, "I had that in my notes," and "That really bothered me too, Gordon." This group is very anti-NRA. Guns are a major 'No-No' in this forum. But let's forget about the guns because Gordon is looking at me now with real regret and sadness in his eyes. "The thing that bothers me the most about your manuscript is the wordiness."

There is an audible intake of air here, as if a giant vacuum has instantly sucked all the oxygen out of the room. Gordon has now accused me of the greatest sin of all...Too many words.

"Let me give you an example." He turns swiftly to the marked page. I notice that the regret and sadness have left his eyes, which now look rather keen. "You have a sentence here, 'Margaret whipped off her Christian Dior panty hose and tied his hairy hands behind his back.'"

Gordon pauses for effect, "Let us never forget the Ernest Hemingway quote, 'The dignity of movement of an iceberg is due to only one-eighth of it being above water.'"

At this point my stomach grows queasy and Gordon recrinkles his sincere squint. "I think you need to examine the worthiness of the words here. Let's take it from the top, let's start with Margaret. Am I the only person who noticed that there were no minority characters in this manuscript?"

"It's set in Minnesota," I say weakly.

"I think the text would be tremendously enhanced by a more American heroine. Let's take some suggestions." After some bickering back and forth over almond creme decaffeinated espresso, the group decides my heroine's name is LaToya Rosita Whitefeather. She's one-third a Woman of Color, one-third Hispanic, and one-third Native American. The conception possibilities boggle my mind.

I notice that Gordon is actually starting to rub his hands together. "Let's get to the verbs. For instance the verb 'whipped.' Isn't that a bit ...well, frothy?" Gordon laughs at his own joke and so does the rest of the group. "Okay, calm down now," he tells them when they get giddy from the ongoing evisceration. To me, they don't look calm at all. They look like they're picking out a tree to throw the rope over.

"What's the next verb? Tied? Okay, whipped and tied. Sounds very S-M, very East Village." They all laugh again at my expense. The next hour is spent with Gordon directing the rewriting of my sentence. It is decided that whipped and tied are verbs that convey entirely too much action. Accordingly less active verbs are agreed upon by a show of hands and when that is a deadlock, by secret ballot. Finally the entire committee-created correct sentence is revealed to me. "LaToya removed her hose and rendered the man actionless."

Stunned, I let the group beat on me for a while with criticisms like "pandering," "tasteless," "clumsy," "immature," "unfocused." I slide back into my Stickley mission style chair, horrified, not by the verbal mugging, but by their taste. How can they rewrite a sentence like 'Margaret whipped off her Christian Dior pantyhose and tied his hairy hands behind his back?' The sentence lives, breathes, and undulates across the page.

And then a surprising thing happens. Gordon calls off the dogs. Like a half-dead deer, I struggle to right myself. I sit up in my chair and work to focus on Gordon's actual words. "Let's all remember that this is pure experimentation," Gordon tells them in his deep, authoritative voice. "Molly has been very brave to venture into this area."

A compliment. I am brave! I wait a moment for my spirit to feel the healing restorative of the one lone compliment. But then I realize that everyone is looking at me for confirmation. "Well..." is the best I can manage. I can't really claim that I wasn't serious. After all, I did write four hundred and twenty pages on Margaret White.

But Gordon carries the ball for me. "You know I've been thinking, Molly. I'm reading at Yale on April twenty-fifth. And I need someone to share the podium with me, kind of warm them up for me. If you were to read selections from your last collection of short stories, I'm sure I could have your name added to the program. I would also like to recommend the stories to my agent."

Gordon has never done even a little favor for me. In fact, he hasn't even been what I would call friendly since he came back from New York. I think that all this time he's suspected that I am a renegade from the program. So why is he helping me now? Is he sorry for me? Or does he just want to keep me within the fold?

I don't know. But I do know that I want to read. This is what I've been hoping for and dreaming about for years. This is recognition, the liberal minimalist elite intelligentsia's gold seal of approval. After sharing the podium with Gordon, I would probably be invited to read at other universities. This could be the beginning of a real career for me. No money of course but a circle of recognition. Recognition. I think about that for a few moments.

Even though extra saliva is forming inside my mouth and my heart is beating in quick shallow beats, there is still a part of me that knows this is the wrong road.

Chapter Six

I know my short stories about unhappy suburban women shoveling snow and raking leaves are lifeless. I know my better work is Margaret White, P.I., who can pull our her 9mm Glock semi-automatic, empty the clip, and then for insurance go to the four-inch throwing knife she keeps in a garter sheath. Margaret White is what I should be reading to a crowd.

Still Gordon has offered me an opportunity, an opportunity for a literary writing career. So I smile graciously at him. "Why thank you. I am available on the twenty-fifth." And I thank my lucky stars that I had the good sense not to retaliate against him for that remark about penis envy.

Sandy follows me out of Rachel's house, bubbling as only a New Age person can bubble. Sandy (her full name is Sandy Brooke. All of those New Age people pick their own names) asks me for a lift. (None of them own cars either.) I am happy to oblige because Sandy wants to go to the Wellness Center where she does massage, and I have been thinking about getting a massage. Actually, I have been thinking about getting a massage for about ten years. It's the bare skin part that stops me, I think.

But since it is my birthday, my attitude is a little different. This attitudinal change was assisted, I believe, by the late birthday gift Dash gave me last year. Approximately two months after my birthday had passed, I found a little white envelope on the kitchen counter. It contained a certificate for cooking lessons at Le Matteaux, our local French eatery, which prepares delicious high calorie food - Dash's kind of food. This gift did not strike me as being especially kind. That was when I made a decision to open up the closed doors of my brain and take a real good look at whatever possibilities I've overlooked.

Since I have several hours before I'm supposed to meet Barb, I drive Sandy to the Wellness Center, a big square white utilitarian building. Sandy insists I come in and when I let her drag me, she hands me the Center's rainbow-colored brochure which lists a diverse array of services considering our geographic location, which is north of most of populated Canada.

Under the category of massage techniques I see that I can choose from therapeutic, Swedish, acupressure, reflexology, polarity and foot reflexology. Or I can go with shiatsu, rolfing, cranio-sacral, reiki, or light and deep tissue work. As long as it comes with nuts and a cherry, I think I'll take it. But wait, there's something more intriguing here - a one hour treatment for food addiction. It's something I'd never do under other circumstances but since it's my birthday and I'm running high from Gordon's offer, my nerve is up.

Recognizing the potential "yes" in me, Sandy expertly maneuvers me into the office of Joan Smith, R.N., B.A., M.A. Despite my initial enthusiasm when I meet Joan, I do hold two things against her. The first is the fact that she has a real name rather than one of those imaginative New Age names like Baby Dancer, Stronge Mann, and Windy Meadows.

The second thing I have against Joan is that she is fat, not just forty pounds overweight like I am, but really fat. I'm sure this is a discriminatory thought on my part against the horizontally challenged. But I figure it's like going to a beautician with bad hair. You think, how good a job is she going to do?

Joan Smith, despite her puritanical name and pork rind body, must be trying to harmonize with the atmosphere here at the Wellness Center because she wears a little name tag with a rainbow on the side, as does everyone else I have seen in this building. I guess it's kind of a team spirit thing, so I give Joan the benefit of the doubt and decide to ignore her lack of imagination and her two-hundred-plus pounds.

From her desk drawer Joan pulls out a detailed consent form. From the careful way she handles the document, I can tell that she thinks this is an important interaction, rather than a bad joke played on us by some liability insurance company.

"We must go through this, point by point," she announces as if she's a Jesuit dealing with a papal encyclical.

I reach for the form. "Let me just sign it."

"Oh no, we have to have an understanding about everything that might happen here."

Oh, for God's sake, I think, what could happen here? Either I lose the weight or I don't, and I really don't feel like wasting a lot of time. "I've already read the form," I lie. "I came in here last week...not for treatment - just to read the form."

"Are you sure you understand the whole thing? Because it's very important that we trust each other, Molly. Hypnosis will not work without trust."

"And hope," I offer.

Joan smiles, "Yes, I suppose that's part of the willing suspension of disbelief. Now, our most common post-hypnotic suggestions are: 'You will eat no fat. You will eat no sugar. You will eat no refined flour.' Does that sound okay?"

"Sure." I'm not here to argue.

Joan leads me into a room that looks like a set from a science fiction movie. The walls are covered with video screens, and a small control console sits in the corner. In the middle of the room is a big comfortable recliner. As I sit in it Joan begins to murmur the baloney I always suspected they used to hypnotize people. She says stuff like "Just relax", and "You're getting sleepier and sleepier." Really, it makes me want to laugh. Besides how am I supposed to relax when I'm so excited at the thought of being revolted by cheeseburgers and irrestibly attracted to asparagus!

Joan must have flipped some switches because wind sounds begin to whisper through the room, the lights dim, and a pattern of swirling blue and purple lines appear on the far wall. "Look at the lights," she commands me in her thin, reedy voice that she is trying to make husky. "Search through your body for points of tension and concentrate on melting them away."

Actually this is a good metaphor for me because I am always sitting in a warm tub with a hot cloth around my neck trying to melt the tension away. Also being a writer, that is a person who deals with fantasy as if it were real, I tend to be very suggestible. In no time at all, I have come to believe that my entire existence is concentrated within the tiny ridge between the big blue line and the little purple one.

Joan's voice is starting to sound kind of warm and friendly, even though she's still speaking that hypnotic mumbo-jumbo stuff, which I eventually stop listening to because I'm way too involved in the action.

You see, I have discovered how to fly.

Sitting in Joan's recliner is no obstacle to my newfound power because I find that the art of flying doesn't actually require a body. Somehow I have learned to slip free of my body and have a really great time free-floating a few feet below the ceiling.

Vaguely, weakly, as if yelling from the end of a football field, I hear Joan ask, "Are you now perfectly peaceful and comfortable?"

I don't respond. It's such a stupid question. Doesn't she know that anyone who has left his or her body is perfectly peaceful and comfortable? Joan tries to talk further with me, but I can't hear her anymore because I have left the room and flown faster than light speed to Beverly Hills, California.

I am in the Dream, which begins as it always does. This is one of the reassuring things about the Dream. I can count on it to be exactly the same every time, a dependable reel of film that someone has so kindly decided to run for me so I wouldn't have to remember all the little details myself. The only thing different about the Dream is that each time there is an increasing pressure and intensity that I can only liken to the last three weeks of pregnancy.

I run through the story slowly and lovingly, hoping for a little more on the end, and I get it. There is a short but delicious period of time when the young Stallone (he looks about twenty-five here) kisses my bald head and then removes my dirty Doc Martin boots and kisses my toes. This is terrific. But when he starts slipping diamond rings onto my toes, I notice that the diamonds cut painfully into the toes next to them. Still, I'm a sport, I put up with it.

Next Sylvester leads me down a long corridor and removes his shirt. This is kind of interesting because the last time I had this dream, I was wondering how his muscles got oiled all by themselves under that silk shirt. Now I can see that nature has given him a little advantage. He has his own self oiling glands. They squirt aromatic oil over the muscles, which jump quickly to that pumped-up state where those ropey veins stand up against the flesh. This is the kind of state that takes other body builders many reps to accomplish. Sylvester obviously has figured out how to do this in a shorter period of time because all he has to do is wave his arms three times in the air while repeating "Kansas, Kansas, Kansas," for those muscles to pump, rope, and oil with charming alacrity.

Sylvester, who is now really looking like an action hero, uses one magnificent oiled and shining arm to open a door and we step into a room full of paper. Stacks and stacks of blank paper.

Again he proposes marriage. Poor fool! Can't he see the obvious - that I am way too much for him. Maddened by desire, he ups his last offer. He wants to give me a prenuptial agreement that nets me in the event of a marriage termination, not only everything that he has ever earned, but everything that he will ever earn. In short, he wishes to mortgage himself to our love.

He gets a little frisky here, to the point that I have had to put him down on the floor to cool his almost frightening ardor and I'm careful to keep my purple Doc Martin boot firmly on his neck. Still I have to admit that I am touched by the sweetness of his offer. After all, even the Duke of Windsor, in giving up the throne for Wallis Simpson, kept an income for himself.

Sylvester looks at me, his velvety eyes wide and pleading. But Joan Smith interrupts us by literally dropping into the room from above, her huge frame held by a Peter Pan harness, her cellophane wings flapping mechanically. "Molly, Molly, Molly...." she calls.

Joan's voice gets louder and Sylvester who up until now has burned with an inhuman brightness, gets fainter and fainter. Almost a ghost, he smiles and waves goodbye as Joan takes over. "Molly, where are you?"

"I'm right here," I answer with obvious annoyance at her unwelcome appearance.

"And where is that?"

"I'm at the party," I tell her. "I'm at Sylvester Stallone's party."

"All right...so you're at a party with Sylvester Stallone..." Joan is speaking so slowly and her voice is so overly calm that I know she is nervous. "...but now Molly, we're going to leave the party."

"But I don't want to leave the party." I can hear the pout in my voice.

However Joan has regained her professional composure. New strength and direction in her voice has made her almost perky. "We're going to think back now to another time...a time when you were a thinner person and you felt very very good. Let's relax and go back in time to that moment."

Although I am in a hypnotized state, there is still no way that I will take orders from a perky voice. The more Joan talks, the less I'm interested, and the further away she sounds. She may think she is controlling me, but I am in another world. Idly I consider her request. While doing this, I fly over the top of the snowy plateau of Tibet, and when the China Sea appears below like a bright mirror, I do a magnificent swan dive into its depths. To my surprise and delight I find that I can breathe in the water just as well as in the air.

But somewhere along the line, I must have acquiesced to the power of her hypnotic command because suddenly I find myself wrenched from the warm sweet waters of the sea and deposited in that most dreaded of all places: the ice rink.

Only it's not our Maine ice rink and everything is different. First of all, I am a different Molly. I'm slender and smooth-skinned and glowing, throbbing with good health, good will, happiness, hope, and excitement. I think I'm young.

And this must be true because sitting next to me in the bleachers is Gail Irwin, who I haven't seen in at least fifteen years. Gail also looks smooth-skinned and pretty even though she's dressed a little slutty. We're at a college hockey game: Boston College vs. Colgate to which Gail has dragged me on a blind date because I owed her for a paper she did for me. Even though I'm a little irritated about being here, you could never figure this out from my body posture, which is basically screaming with youthful energy and brainless joy as I watch my first hockey game.

"Barbaric!" I announce to Gail, who has a different response.

"These guys are all hunks," she declares, an overabundance of saliva threatening to slide from her lower lip.

"They're animals!" I counter. "They're like ...football players." It's the worst thing I can think of to say.

Directly in front of us, two players collide against the glass, creating a loud crunching thud. It is the first time I have ever heard this noise. The fans are screaming so I have to raise my voice to speak to Gail and I begin to wonder what I have let myself in for date-wise. "Which one is mine?"

"That one," she points.

When Dashiel Lemeiux Denton first comes into my line of sight, he is skating along looking up into the stands but when he sees that we are watching him, he makes a speed stop and twirls the stem of his hockey stick so that the blade spins like a pinwheel. He follows this gesture by skating madly down the ice, shoulders swaying, legs pumping, and seconds later he scores with a wrist shot into the upper left hand corner. Ever so slightly, completely unconsciously, and independent of the rest of my bodily functions, my heart increases it's beat.

Later as Gail and her date and I wait outside the locker room I feel... something. An atmospheric change? A drop in humidity? An increase in electrical energy? I don't know. But when Dash walks out of the changing room, the light intensifies. I know this because I am right here and I am not drunk and I can see that the light has brightened.

We look at each other...for too long. Neither one of us wants to break the spell. Gail and her boyfriend stop looking at each other and stare at us instead. Then the boyfriend says softly, "Coup de foudre!"

I look at Dash now, knowing, although I did not know then, the translation for the French expression for love at first sight - It is the clap of thunder.

Watching this now, I recognize the moment when the bolt of lightning strikes. I can feel this in every atom in my body. Then from across years, and ceremonies, and births and death, I hear the little thin inconsequential voice of Joan Smith calling me back. But I don't want to go back.

Joan speaks authoritatively about visualizing the food I will eat and her voice grows louder and stronger with each word. She tells me that when I see the food I will visualize the globules of fat within the food. From a distance I hear a tinny bell. Then she begins to talk about visualizing the sugar. I hear that tinny ringing again, growing louder. And while she talks, all I can think about is the clap of thunder, the feel of the air, the excitement that fills every cell of my body, the sheer thrill of being there. And all I want, and maybe all I ever wanted was for it to last - forever.

Chapter Seven

"Happy Birthday!" Barb's well made-up face eases into a smile.

I'm a little late but Barb has saved me a seat next to her at the table. Of course, we have the best table in the room; right next to the big windows, right next to the sign that reads, "Welcome Bangor Ladies Luncheon Club. A Marvelous Maine Spring is here." We're all ignoring the fact that even though it's March another five inches of snow fell yesterday.

Sometimes I wonder why Barb keeps bringing me here. At the eight tables in the small dining room is the club - a collection of well-groomed, hard-eyed babes wearing soft camouflage clothing like DKNY and Nicole Miller. And although the hair is softly and expertly done and the vocal tones are modulated, underneath it all, the same heart beats in every chest - for this is the den of the warrior women.

I try really hard at these luncheons, to keep up a front, to not say anything or do anything to give myself away. For example, I never admit that I bring my husband coffee in the morning (when I'm not mad at him) or that I have allowed my sons to have twenty friends sleep over in the family room (resulting in a bill of three hundred dollars to repair the damaged walls) that I have to ask, no beg, my husband to take me to the movies and even then all I ever get to see are war movies (I have seen every Vietnam movie made, including <u>Hamburger Hill</u> and <u>Full Metal Jacket</u>).

Here at the club, I try to pretend I am one of them. I act like a gal who makes jokes about her husband behind his back, who arranges the weekend's social plans with her girlfriends and then lets her husband know what functions he's accompanying her to at the end of the week. But it's hard, let me tell you. One slip and in an instant any one of them would make me for the weakling I am.

This is my third luncheon and so far they have accepted me as Barb's protegee. I know this cover can only last for so long, but by weighing every word and not talking too much, I have made it so far. Sometimes I wonder why I even come here, since I have to work so hard at fitting in. I think maybe it's a control issue. They have it, I want it.

Patty Lotito turns to me casually and asks, "What'd ya get for your birthday, Molly?" While I hesitate, Patty fills in for me. "A Mercedes, a fur?" Patty is only three months out of Long Island. She has a really garish accent and still wears leather jackets with studs. Although she dresses differently from the others, having not been here long enough to pick up the New England dress code, Patty exhibits the most important quality for admission to the inner circle...balls.

Obviously I can't answer truthfully here. Imagine the reaction if I told them Dash didn't even remember my birthday - They'd probably throw me a pity party. The way I see it, I have no alternative here but to lie. And there is one thing I've learned about lying. Never lie little - lie big. For some reason, it's more believable.

"Dash gave me a trip," I tell them and this is greeted with a hushed murmur of approval.

But Patty keeps probing. "Is he taking you on a cruise, or something?"

"No, I'm traveling alone." I say making up the story as I go along. "I'm traveling West to a film festival thing on the relevance of the Ancient Roman Empire." I always try to use my teaching and university degrees around them. It tends to shut them up.

"Oh," Patty says and concentrates on the basket of rolls that has just been placed in front of her. When I watch her pull apart a roll and coat the inside with butter. I hear a tinny little bell, followed by the words, "You will not eat fat!" and "You will not eat flour!" intoned by a voice that sounds an awful lot like Charlton Heston in that movie, The Ten Commandments. I'm so startled that I look around to see where it came from. Patty tries to pass the basket of rolls to me, but my hand recoils involuntarily, and she passes them to Anne Chamberlain, an older but very well maintained member.

Barb leans over the table conspiratorily. "Don't look now, but wasn't that Karen Bender?"

"Where?" Heck, I'm still looking around for Charlton Heston.

"Our waitress," Barb sounds annoyed. "Don't look at her." I do as Barb commands and lower my gaze to the table, careful not to look at the rolls.

But Anne Chamberlain who speaks in the loud stage voice of an aging actress, insists, "Karen Bender can't be waitressing here. She's a member."

"Not anymore," Barb leans forward on her elbows and says knowledgeably, "Six months ago she threw Patrick out." A simultaneous muted "no" echoes around the table.

"I also heard that he's stiffing her on the money. Obviously that rumor is true." Barb reaches into the roll basket and makes a selection. (All these women exercise two hours a day and can eat whatever they want.) As I watch her pull apart the roll, I feel a wave of nausea rise in my throat.

"How many children do they have?" Anne asks, always one for a good groan.

"Three," Barb spreads the butter. "Uh-oh, here she comes." Barb, Anne, and Patty studiously drop their eyes to their laps or fiddle with their purses as Karen arrives with the lunch. But I say hello to Karen. She looks tired, and the expensive streak job in her hair is growing out, but other than that she seems fine. Karen looks relieved that someone has spoken to her. Barb, Anne, and Patty retrieve themselves from rifling through their purses and make a big show of not having noticed Karen and then another big show of greeting her. Barb even tells her that her hair looks good, which is not actually true. Meanwhile Karen serves the club luncheon platter.

"What's this?" I ask Barb because it doesn't look good. It looks all red and icky.

"Raspberry quiche," she tells me and this brings on a ringing in my head like that tinnitis I sometimes get from taking too many aspirins. And Charlton Heston has crawled into my ear with a megaphone. "You will not eat fat, You will not eat flour, You will not eat sugar," he announces ominously.

This alone would be startling enough but my reaction to the food is another surprise. It sickens me, repulses me, it looks like garbage from a dumpster. And then I get it - The hypnosis worked.

Good old Joan Smith has actually done the trick for me. It's thin city coming up in the next few months. It's sarong skirts, and minis, and little white short shorts. I look at Barb-the-Bone digging into her quiche and wonder if I could actually get thinner than her. Trying to control my excitement I ask Karen for some coffee, which she gets me and then retreats. Fortunately there are no bells or Charlton Heston announcements at the cup of black coffee, and I drink it down greedily.

Patty licks raspberry sauce from the tines of her fork. "So why is Patrick Bender being so cheap?" she asks, bringing us back to the news of the day.

"It's routine," Barb loves to explain things. "It's what men do when they don't want to pay. They countersue and ask for child custody." She dabs her lips with her napkin. "Karen never had proper control over him," she says disdainfully.

"Are the kids in therapy?" Patty asks.

"If they're not, they will be. I hear he's refusing to agree to any college money. It's a power trip that some men get off on. They like the kids to beg for an education...kind of like feudal lords in the Middle Ages." Barb curls her lips into a Tina Turner sneer before noticing that I haven't eaten anything. "Are you on another diet again?" she asks me.

"No," I tell her, thinking that technically you wouldn't call this a diet.

Patty shakes her head and reaches for another roll. "Sounds like she married a louse."

"Patrick was educable," Barb explains. "But Karen was always too sensitive for her own good. God save us from sensitive people. The worst thing is that her kids will be the ones to suffer." At this point everyone nods their heads because after all, this is a universal truth.

"Patrick will run through a succession of girlfriends. Eventually there will be a stepmother who will, of course, hate the children. But I can't say I feel sorry for Karen because in some ways she brought it on herself."

I wonder if maybe I've misheard some part of this narrative, "Barb, correct me if I'm wrong but wasn't Patrick Bender screwing everything that walked?"

"Only his secretaries. They were always redheads and he changed them every two years. Karen should have gotten a bottle of hair dye."

Patty throws her napkin down on the tablecloth in a show of disgust. "If my husband was stupid enough to have an affair, I'd hold onto him

31

and punish him for the rest of his life. He would never get done making that up to me."

Barb pats her hand, "I'm so glad you joined our group." Anne agrees, "She's adorable."

But I sip my black coffee and wonder at this embracement of misery for the sake of a satisfactory revenge. What about the old adage, 'Living well is the best revenge'? I fail to see how punishing your husband within the prison of a dead marriage can be considered living well.

So I make the dangerous decision to float a trial balloon. "Has anybody considered the possibility that Karen Bender just got completely and totally disgusted with her life?"

Chapter Eight

The airline clerk was wrong - You can get from Bangor, Maine to Los Angeles in one day. All you have to do when you arrive at a new airport is take the very next plane that's heading south or west. It's a little expensive but I figure Dash can worry about that.

I arrive at L.A.X. a/k/a Los Angeles Airport on what they tell me is a bad day. Still it is so bright that I have to slip on the big sunglasses that I had the foresight to buy on one of my stop overs, wherever it was, Atlanta, Chicago, Denver, I can't remember. The temperature is a perfect seventy-two degrees, and the first thing I do upon entering the terminal is ditch my heavy winter coat. Actually I give it to a homeless person, but this being L.A., she throws it in the trash.

Next I go to the taxi stop and eyeball the drivers. I pass up the shifty-eyed short one, walk by the big stupid one, not because I don't like big and stupid but because I think maybe his English isn't so good and I'm going to need a driver I can talk to: somebody who looks like he knows his way around - basically I need Mr. California.

So I settle on a tall Nordic type who looks just like a Ken doll. Actually, he's such a match for Ken he makes you wonder if he has smooth plastic genitals under his pants.

When I get into his cab, there is a loud protest from the other drivers because the Ken doll is not first in line. But I motion him to drive and he does. I know from his cab license that his name is Todd Johnson which suits him. However Todd hasn't said a word since we pulled away from arrivals. And I was hoping for a loose chatty kind of guy. Realizing that

I am going to have to take over, I do so. "Do you know where Sylvester Stallone lives?"

Todd cranes his neck to look at me while still driving. With his light gray eyes and well-planed face, he really is handsome in a male model kind of way. "Sure," he says after again facing forward so he can see the road. "Out here we've got maps of the stars, and the tour buses go by twice a day. Everybody knows where Sylvester lives."

Wonderful - I settle back in my seat as he drives past rows of palm trees and then the beautiful little towns along the Pacific. Todd assures me that he is not padding his fare but that this way is really quicker because the average freeway speed at this time of day is twenty-two mph and that no one in his or her right mind gets on the freeway unless absolutely, absolutely necessary.

He also tells me that he's an actor from Ohio and that he's been out here for ten years. He explains to me how hard it is for someone like him (who represents the Nordic Midwestern look) to get work in the New Hollywood. According to Todd, all the good parts are going to short dark ethnic guys, especially the Hispanics and American Indians. Andy Garcia and Keanu Reeves, he tells me, are really not good actors.

Finally at Santa Monica, he begins to cut over along Wilshire, toward Beverly Hills. As we near it I am stunned by the unreality of the place. Not only does it look like you could literally eat off the street (In Maine the streets are dirty nine months of the year) but everything is so perfect, nothing out of place, and the light.... The light is so completely different from the dark gulag I have left behind that there is the definite feeling that I have entered a new world.

And the houses! One mansion after another, each in a completely different style; Tudor, Western ranch, Spanish, Neo-Gothic, creating the eclectic look of a subdivision planned by a drunken crossdresser on a friendly bet.

When Todd finally pulls up to the biggest estate and announces, "Sylvester Stallone," I am not disappointed. A huge white columned mansion with Neo-Gothic columns in the Corinthian style with magnificent landscaping is surrounded an eight-foot fence with iron gates. Several burly men with size nineteen necks are engaged in a leg wrestling contest on the front lawn. Watching them are at least a dozen rottweilers.

They cavort lazily on grass that is neon chartreuse in color. I take off my sunglasses to see if these colors are real and this is when it hits me.

I have dreamed the right mansion! This is the exact same house that I have seen night after night in my dreams. An enormous adrenaline surge pulsates through my bloodstream and I struggle to control the elation and excitement I feel. I know that sometime later I'm going to have to think through this proof of my psychic or prescient ability and work it into my belief system. However, things are just too busy for that right now.

I slide my sunglasses back on because the neon brightness of the sunlight bouncing off the grass of the front lawn is too much for me. As I slip the glasses into place, I realize, despite my growing excitement, that I have a problem.

"How am I going to get in?" I ask Todd.

"Beats me," Todd shrugs, unaware that he has, by virtue of being my cab driver, accepted the obligation of solving all my immediate problems.

"But seriously," I continue. "How do you call on someone who has a gate?"

Todd cranes his neck around again so he can get a better view of me. "Well, you just don't call on Sylvester Stallone," he says rather slowly.

"So the gate and the dogs are buffers." I think out loud. "Stallone is insulating himself from the public."

"Of course," Todd looks at me as if he's worried I'm a crazed and dangerous fan and I notice he keeps one hand on the door handle. "Sylvester Stallone is a very big star," Todd instructs me.

"I know that."

Todd licks his lips and then paints a fake smile on his good looking kisser. "Are you getting out?"

"I don't know."

"When will you know?" he asks patiently.

I eye Todd. Even though he doesn't exactly seem like a film connected Hollywood kind of guy, even though what he seems to be is a guy who with the help of a Dale Carnegie course could maybe park cars at Spago, he is my only source of information. "How would one go about meeting Sylvester Stallone?" I ask.

Todd sighs. I guess he's made a gratuity motivated decision to humor me. "That would depend upon why I wanted to meet him."

"I have a story for him."

Todd's expression changes from fear to relief and he laughs. "Geez, I thought you were some kind of nut, but you're just a writer."

I feel a little insulted at this. Are writers so wimpy that they can't even be in the crazed and dangerous category? "A writer can be a nut," I tell him stubbornly.

"Naaah," he says, still laughing.

"What about the woman who broke into Steven King's house claiming that he stole the original manuscript of Misery from her apartment?"

"Is that true?"

"Yes."

"Okay, so maybe there's one nut, but I'm a writer, and so is my roommate and so is my brother.... Everybody out here is either an actor or a writer or both, and everybody has a script. I'll tell you what to do."

I smile... at last, some helpful advice.

"You register the script with the Guild. Then you send the script around to agents because no sane development person is going to read anything that comes in cold."

"I'm not going to do that."

"Why not?"

"I'm going to deal with Stallone personally."

"Okay," Todd looks over at Stallone's gate. "Then I guess you want to get out here."

Hmmm, I realize that pounding on that gate will surely bring the rottweilers and the guys with the nineteen inch necks and that doesn't seem like a good way to meet Stallone. This is when I decide that I have to forget normal channels and find the odd irregular route. "Where does the Stallion like to eat?" I ask Todd. "Where does he work out? Where does he get his haircut? Where does he buy his shoes?"

"I don't know. I'm not the president of his fan club. And I've got to take some other fares, you know," Todd tells me.

"All right," I make a quick decision. "Take me to the place where you think I'm most likely to meet him."

Todd puts the cab in drive and shakes his head. He's beginning to look annoyed but he drives into Westwood to a small bar next to a big gymnasium. "I've heard that some of the action guys who work out at Le Jock, L.A. like to drink here."

I look at the sign above the door. It's small and old and reads, "Tony's Roadhouse."

"Who shall I ask for?"

Todd gives me a big smile, like he's happy to be rid of me, "Ask for Tony," he says.

Chapter Nine

Before I step inside the bar, I take a deep breath. The air is warm and fresh and a slight wind rattles the fronds of the nearby palms. Not being accustomed to entering strange bars in foreign places, I'm kind of nervous. So I take another deep breath for luck, before stepping into the darkness.

Tony's is one of those exclusively macho places I usually try to avoid. The floor is dark and wooden and photographs of old time boxing greats cover the walls; Joe E. Louis, Jack Dempsey, Sugar Ray Robinson.

The bar is long, dark, and oiled, like the clientele I expect. Behind the bar on top of the counter is a big jar of pickled eggs. I wonder who in Southern California actually eats pickled eggs? I decide it doesn't matter. It's a decor thing.

At the far end of the bar are two really strange-looking guys. The younger one must be about 6'6" and rail thin. His long hippie hair is straggly and he wears beaded bracelets on his wrists. On his left bicep he has a tattoo of a coiled snake while his right bicep shows off the image of a big pair of red lips. The short bald guy next to him is making a necklace from a canvas sack full of antique soda can pop-tops. But I concentrate on the bartender who's an older guy with a crinkly, well-tanned face, lots of unruly white hair, and brown eyes he thinks are sexy. I know this from the way he leers at me. Since I haven't been leered at in quite a while, I don't quite know how to handle it.

"What'll it be, Doll?"

I review my options, careful to remember the tinny bells that go off in my ears when I make a mistake. This is not hard to recall since they went off all across the country whenever I was offered airplane food. So I say, "Diet coke."

"You don't want a diet coke. You want a frozen daiquiri or a mint julep or a golden cadillac."

Ordinarily I would hate that kind of response, but I'm on a mission, so I smile. "I don't really want anything. I'm just looking for somebody."

"Bartenders never get chatty until after they take the order. It's in the Bartenders Code of Ethics and Responsibility."

"Okay, give me a frozen daiquiri," I tell him even though I know it's made with sugar and I won't be able to drink it.

"We don't have a blender."

I look around the place. "You probably can't make a mint julep either."

My nemesis nods his head like a bad little boy. "We're fresh out of mint."

"So what do you have?"

"Shot and a beer."

I sigh. "Okay, set me up. You can drink the shot and I'll try to drink the beer even though I hate beer."

"You got it now." He pours the shot into a glass and the beer into a mug, which I note is neither cold nor clean, and he puts them in front of me on the long scarred wooden bar. Why do I feel like I'm in the middle of a Mafia movie? I don't know, but since I do, I put a twenty on the bar as if I'm going to be drinking for a while. "So where can I find Tony?" I ask casually.

He takes the twenty to the register and puts my change on the bar. "You're looking at him, Doll." He crinkles up his leathery face into a smile and downs his shot. Then he leans over the bar and fingers the lapel of my suit jacket. "Love the suit, Doll. What is that, velvet? We don't see much velvet around here."

This guy smells like a hundred-year-old brewery, and I suspect it's not his breath. I think it's coming up out of his skin, but I'm committed here, so I keep trying. "Actually I came down here looking for Sylvester Stallone. I guess that sounds pretty silly." Having determined his type by virtue of his fondling my jacket lapels, I actually lower my head and look up at him a la Princess Diana. I can tell from the grin that he loves it.

"That's not silly," he tells me. "That's what all the tourists say."

"I'm not a tourist."

"Yeah, you really look like a local in that velvet suit," Tony smiles. "You've got to understand, Doll, that Stallone is not just a star. He's a mega-star. He has to have people who talk to the people who want to talk to him. Sure, he is one of my nearest and dearest friends. And sure, he is a great guy. But when you have thousands of fans and great fame, you're forced to make some lifestyle changes. Take me, for example."

"Take you?"

"Hell, in this town I'm an even bigger celebrity than Sylvester. Didn't you know they made a movie about me?"

"I'm sorry, I didn't know."

"It's about how I had to run from the mob in the forties. It didn't gross high, but it's well known in all the literary film circles, which is satisfaction enough for me. Personally I've never cared about making a lot of money."

"Great."

But Tony laughs. "I'm bullshitting you, Doll. That's Rule Number Two of the Bartenders Code of Ethics and Responsibility."

Well, I've tried to play along with this guy and gotten nowhere, so I figure the only thing left to do is throw myself on his mercy. "Look I've just got to meet Sylvester Stallone. He's rolling around inside my head. It's gotten so bad I'm actually dreaming about him."

"Sylvester! That dirty dog. You're actually dreaming about Stallone?"

I nod, feeling both miserable and embarrassed.

"He's an actor, for God's sake."

"He's not just an actor, Tony. He's also a writer."

Tony chuckles. "Look, Doll. I love the guy. But let's be straight here. He's not a writer. He's a screenwriter."

Now, I'm not trying to nominate Stallone for a jury at the Cannes Film Festival. Sure I've had fun at his movies but I'm an overeducated university-trained minimalist writer. Until the Dream arrived I never even thought about Sylvester Stallone. Unfortunately for me, however, the dream brought with it a compelling fascination, maybe even a brain fever because I just have to see Stallone in the flesh.

"Tony, Stallone isn't just an actor and writer." I try to convey a sense of urgency by my tone of voice. "He's also a director, a painter, a collector of serious art. He's actually a modern day .... Renaissance man." When I see I'm getting nowhere with Tony I finally give it all up and just beg. "All I know is that I <u>have</u> to meet him because I know that when I meet him, my life will change."

Tony leans forward like he's going to give me some important information. "Doll," he says, reeking of Scotch, "I've been behind this bar for many years, and I've seen a lot of interesting situations, so I'd like to give you the benefit of my life's experience."

"Okay," I say slowly.

"You've heard of the expression, 'Hold onto your dreams.'"

"Sure." I smile at him, I know he's on my side now.

"Dump them, Doll. Dump them fast. Get all that shit out of your head. Only when you do that can you get up in the morning and really see the day."

I probably look like I'm on twenty-second delay because I don't get this. Not only won't he help me, but is he also telling me to give up?

"You go down to Venice Beach and get a job in one of those little t-shirt shops. You watch the sun set over the Pacific every night, and then you come in here. I'll straighten you out. Tony Lamboni, Philospher King of L.A. You just put Sylvester Stallone out of your head."

I don't know what to say. For the first time I realize how completely alone I am, how far from home ...how hungry.

The two guys at the end of the bar get up and come over to me. The short bald one is holding his finished pop-top necklace, which he now presents to me, as an Hawaiian lei.

"It's a tribute," Tony tells me. "Every day Lucky makes one of those and gives it to the most miserable-looking tourist."

I get up from the stool. "You can have the beer," I tell Tony.

"Don't go drinking anything with fruit or flowers sticking out the top and stay away from those amino acid smart drinks. You want a real drink, you come on back to Tony."

I smile weakly and head for the front door. Dusted, I realize, I'm dusted. As I step outside, I notice that right in front of Tony's, there's a bench for the bus stop. And since I have nothing else to do, I sit down and wait for a while. But no buses come, and nobody else comes by to wait for a bus. Comfortable on the bench, I think the temperature is ...well, perfect and I can't help wonder about what it is like now in Northeastern

Maine, where you can get a wicked case of frostbite just waiting for a bus like this. Across the street at Le Jock, L.A., an unending stream of Maseratis, Mercedes, and Range Rovers transport an amazing number of good-looking men to the health club. I continue watching as the tall hippie and the short bald guy from Tony's Roadhouse come out, climb into a big white limo, drive across the street, park in front of Le Jock, L.A., exit the limo, and go into the building.

Now I have a hard time believing that those two went in there to exercise. I figure they're either messengers or they went there to pick up somebody, which does suggest that right across the street in that building, there are important Hollywood celebrities. So I decide to check it out.

When I stroll past the big white limo, I notice the plate reads SS#1. Could the limo actually belong to Sylvester Stallone? It sounds impossible but after all I did manage to dream his actual mansion in precise detail without ever seeing it.

I push through the double glass doors into a dark, lush, and exclusively male health club. This makes me pause because it had not occurred to me that this might be a place that prohibited women. I wonder with slight irritation if this is legal and even if it is, then why hasn't somebody done something about it. I pretend to make a call from the pay phone near the entrance, but really I'm stalling for time, summoning my nerve.

I focus on the important lesson I learned when I turned thirty-eight. That was the year I realized I had become invisible to the male population. The experience felt rather Ray Bradbury, kind of like walking through a hidden window into another dimension where men can not see me but middle-aged women and very young children can. There are a few special circumstances however that allow men to see me such as if I threaten them or scream. My friend Barb tells me that it happens to every woman at some unspecified point between the ages of 38-45, unless you have surgery. She tells me that men also reach an age when they become invisible. That age, however, is 85-90 years old.

At first this cultural phenomenon bothered me, because when I lost my visibility, I felt a part of my humanity had been taken from me. However I slowly began to adjust to my new social position and eventually came to realize that there are a few advantages to this. I began to see that what originally distressed me could even become a powerful transformation because...an invisible woman can't make a mistake. You cannot embarrass an invisible woman. In fact, an unafraid unembarrassable invisible woman can do ... anything she wants.

Boldly I push past the young male receptionist who fulfills my expectations by failing to notice me. Confidently I stride past the men entering rooms to play squash. To them I am just a whisper of air.

Ahead of me in the corridor is that tall tattoed hippie from Tony's Roadhouse, and surprisingly he <u>does</u> notice me. This is troubling because to pierce the invisibility veil, I must present some kind of threat and how could I possibly be threatening to this tough-looking man? Still he has a nervous look on his face as he hurries away from me. So like Margaret White, my private eye, I make a quick decision to follow him.

Chapter Ten

Since the tattooed man is cutting through the pool area, I pick up a few towels as extra camouflage in the unlikely event there is some stray mutant who is actually capable of noticing a woman forty years old. I know that carrying towels immediately puts me in the category of servant, but this is a category with which I am intimately acquainted and a disguise I can assume with ease. Now, since I am in complete disguise in an area filled with handsome tanned muscled naked men, I make sure I take a really good long look.

Exiting the pool area, I follow my target up some stairs and down another corridor. The tattooed man is just ahead of me now and has entered a small room. As I follow him in, I see a naked man lying on his stomach on the black leather massage table. I let my eyes slide up the well muscled back that looks slightly familiar to the dark hair on the back of the head which is by now definitely familiar. It's him!

Sylvester Stallone raises himself up on one elbow and the tattooed man whispers in his ear. Sylvester immediately pulls a towel around his lower body, gets up, and begins backing cautiously away from me. "Nice necklace," he says as he opens the door behind him and makes a fast exit. The tattooed man grabs Stallone's clothes and together they hightail it out of Le Jock, L.A.

I try to follow, but two burly masseurs block my way for long enough so that when I run out the back door, all I see is the big white limo speeding away. Now another woman might call this a failure or be embarrassed. But I say you can't be embarrassed when you're invisible and this was no failure. Because there was a moment when Sylvester looked at me - he even spoke to me - and it felt exactly like the dream.

Heart pounding, I decide to leave the general area of Le Jock, L.A. just in case some overly cautious, anal retentive security guard decides to call the police. Luckily I find a cab and head back to the airport. Not because I'm quitting, but because I have honed my plan, and I know that this hard target can be hit.

Fortunately there is space available on a flight back home. The bigger piece of luck, however, is that the airline clerk actually accepts my credit card which means that Dash hasn't cancelled it yet.

When I arrive at the Bangor airport, they're just plowing out from a new four-inch spring snowfall. The timing of my arrival is perfect because I only have to kill a half hour drinking coffee at the airport restaurant to be sure that Dash and the boys have actually left the house. Then I take a cab back to the four bedroom center hall colonial I used to call home.

Looking out the window of the taxi as the driver pulls into my subdivision I see new snow artfully draped over the drooping boughs of the evergreens and young mothers outside making snowmen with their toddlers. Obviously they don't know what a hell hole this place really is.

After paying the driver, I am tempted to go next door to Barb's house because at this moment if there's anybody in the world I want to talk to it's her and it's a wickedly powerful temptation. But I have a suspicion that if I were to go over there, I would still be talking to Barb at 3:15 when my sons come home from school and that somehow they would lure me back to the house to cook for them. Then Dash would come home and without saying much, grouchily accept my brief absence, and in the end, I would be quietly sucked down into the quicksand of my former life. So I fight my desire to see Barb, get out my keys, and slip into my empty house.

God, it's a mess. It's hard to believe that one man and four boys can totally destroy a place in so short a time. But the plan here is not to clean up. The plan here is to get what I need and get out. I'm not going to use the toilet, I'm not going upstairs for my summer clothes, and I'm not opening the refrigerator - especially the refrigerator.

However it does occur to me as I walk past the double doors of the big white refrigerator that it might be nice to leave a note. This is something I have fantasized about doing for years, probably because it makes such a statement. You don't want to leave a note by the phone, you don't want to leave a note on the bed, you leave it where the man will find it - on the refrigerator.

So I pick up a pen and a slip of paper. But what to write? "Adios, you bad guy. Hasta la vista, Baby." I don't know, that just doesn't convey the right tone. Besides as a writer I have a tendency to edit anything I've written, five seconds after it's hit the page, and everything I think of sounds so .... well, bitter. And bitter, no matter how you arrange it, is not attractive.

So I decide to go with the utter truth. I write, "Away on business, Molly. P.S. I am taking Victor." I tack it up on the big white frost free Amana. It's perfect; short, brusque, vague, and does not specify the length of my absence.

I laugh and take the van keys from the row of hooks in the hallway. I am careful not to look down at any of the hockey equipment strewn along the wallboard, because I am afraid there may be a wellstream of emotion that has not been destroyed. However, the sad-eyed hamsters are not something I can ignore, especially poor pregnant Sergei Federov. So I get out the bag of food and pour some into the dishes, and wonder when, if ever, the boys will remember to feed these animals. The answer to this question leads me to an irresistible impulse.

I grab the bag of pellets, pick up the hamster cages, and head outside. Like a trusty companion, Victor waits for me; big, safe, reliable. Victor is the reason I have flown across the country for the second time in twenty-four hours, because in addition to the fact that Victor is my friend, Victor allows me to do something that is critical to my plan. Victor allows me to live on the same street as Sylvester Stallone.

I step up, climb in, and drive out of Maine and across Canada on Route 17. This is always the best route West because you can drive so much faster in Canada. I have never figured out the conversion of kilometers to miles but I do know that when I am cruising the Queen's Expressway at 83 mph, the Royal Canadian Mountie patrol car will speed by me in pursuit of some other guy who's really speeding.

We drive forever - at least that's how it feels; hours on the highway, followed by coffee breaks at the truckstops. Whenever I get tired I just pull Victor off the highway, lock up and sleep. Everyday we end up a little farther West than the day before.

Eventually just before Victor and the hamsters and I reach Moose Jaw, we drop down out of Canada and into North Dakota, where we head for the Badlands so I can buy a pair of red cowboy boots, and a new pair of black jeans since my old ones seem to be falling off of me.

By the time I've left Montana and am heading for Big Sky, Idaho, I have a trucker's tan on my left arm and my cowboy boots are dusty and worn. We drive and drive, just Victor and me and the big blue sky. Well, that and the C.B. radio, which places a world of information at my fingertips. In my head, I've plotted out several stories from tips and advice I've gotten from truckers, who I have discovered are mainly action/ adventure buffs.

Whenever I take a break from driving, which isn't too often since I have discovered that trucker's panacea, No-Doz, I sit outside in the sun and eat fruit, mostly oranges and lemons. This is how I sustain myself nutritionally without setting off the bells in my head. One day while sitting on a sunny rock, I get an urge to cut my hair, so I find an old pair of scissors in the back of the van and do it. It looks like hell but it sure feels good and I like to run my fingers through the uneven layers. The further west I drive, the better I feel.

In Idaho, I begin heading South, and cut down into Oregon, which is where Sergei Federov has her babies; two sweet little pups, I name after old-time hockey greats, Gordy Howe and Rocket Richard.

And then... California. I maneuver Victor onto treacherous Route 1 on a day when the wind is up along the Pacific and I have to keep a firm hold on the wheel as we swerve along the cliff's edge. The driving is made even more difficult by kids in black Mercedes convertibles speeding at us from the opposite direction. Their long blond hair flies in the breeze as they whip around the road's edge.

Poor Victor, my good horse, is tired and dirty by the time we close in on Los Angeles. But I keep him going until we turn onto Eldorado Avenue and have Sylvester's mansion in sight. Fortunately it's dusk as we pull up and park. The rottweilers and bodyguards take no notice of us, and Victor and I turn in early. I sleep the good sleep, knowing that tomorrow - my new life begins.

Chapter Eleven

The day begins early at Casa Stallone. Around seven o'clock, the sprinklers go off, showering the entire compound with a light rain. Shortly after eight, men arrive to service the estate. Three gardeners appear, one for the grass, the other for the flowering bushes, a third for the giant palms. Then the pool man comes with his van and his assistant. A dog trainer dressed head to toe in black kevlar arrives with a dummy to conduct attack drills. This is followed by a dimensionally well-matched pair of exercise trainers who set up on the south lawn for an aerobics program for the bodyguards and miscellaneous staff.

Eventually the aerobicizing bodyguard contingency notices me, and one of the group is deputized to question me. I am sitting quite comfortably in my club chair in Victor's midsection sipping my mocha cappuccino (skim milk only) made from the built-in espresso machine, when the bodyguard taps on the window, "Ya gotta move the van," he says.

I open the side door and invite him in, knowing that he can smell the coffee and can't fail to notice that on my built-in T.V., Montel Williams is attacking the subject of steroid abuse. All of this has caught his attention but he is a good soldier. He refuses to enter my sanctum sanctorum and repeats his command to move the van.

"No can do, amigo." I tell him and wait for my brusque dismissal of his physical presence to sink in. But he just gives me a quizzical look, probably because he can't process that kind of refusal from a 5'3" woman.

"Ya gotta move the van," he says for the third time.

"Look, pal, I'm on a stakeout and I'm gonna be here at least a week but this is government business and absolutely confidential."

"Well," he says slowly, "I have to report to my boss who you're with."

"Federal government."

He's unimpressed.

"Special branch. We used to be called B.A.T.F."

He still doesn't get it.

"Bureau of Alcohol, Tobacco and Firearms."

This finally impresses him and he nods and moves away.

"What's your name?" I ask.

He stops, then swivels his head around on his massive neck, "Trip."

"Is that short for Tripoli?"

He gives me a crooked half smile. "Yeah."

"No kidding. I had an Uncle Tripoli," I lie. "Where're you from?" Any Italian knows what this question means. It doesn't mean did you grow up in Brooklyn or Jersey or Boston? It means which province in Italy do your ancestors come from?

"Calabria," he answers.

"Beautiful area," I tell him. "Come back and talk to me once in a while. It gets lonely on stakeout."

"Okay."

"But don't tell anybody."

He nods.

"And, Trip, every now and then when I have to leave, will you make sure nobody else parks here? I need to have this exact spot for the electronics equipment."

"Sure." A few hours later after no Sylvester sightings, I leave to do a few errands. Victor needs a bath, so I take him to a do-it-yourself car wash. Then I take Victor to the gas station for some fuel and an oil change and me to the supermarket to stock up on fruit and oranges.

The supermarkets out here are amazing. I happily discover enormous sections of food that don't set off the bells in my head. It seems as though eighty percent of the supermarkets here are free of "Fat, flour, and sugar." I stock up the van and then ask where I can find an Italian food store. Although it seems I have to drive forever to get to La Casa Nostra, it is worth it because they have exactly what I want in their specialty section. Then I head back to Sylvester's.

Loyal Tripoli has saved my parking spot. He is fooling around with his bodyguard friends teasing the dogs on the front lawn. I have a feeling they do that alot and wonder if they have all their fingers. I drive into my pre-assigned spot, and quickly set up a little surprise for Trip. Then I stick my head out the van window and call him to come over. This time he is willing to come into Victor. And I know it's because of the smell. On the little fold-out table, I have placed a steaming plate of the Calabrians' favorite macaroni, cavadells. "You've got to eat the whole thing. I'm too full to help out," I tell him.

Trip practically inhales the macaroni. "Where'd you find them?" he asks when he finally surfaces from the dish.

I tell him, "My mother's Italian" Another lie.

"Aah," he sighs and I know that we are now bonded for life.

I offer him a cup of cappuccino which he accepts an while I am steaming the milk, I ask, "Trip, have you noticed any suspicious behavior on the part of any of the neighbors?"

He thinks about that for a moment. I can see he's having trouble shifting gears into a suspicious modality. After all when you've just eaten the food of your genetic heritage it's hard to be anything but expansive. Trip screws up his face, as evidence that he is thinking hard. "Maybe that Mary Pat Johanssen. Maybe she's been up to something."

I did not know that Mary Pat Johanssen, the New Age guru to the stars, lived on this street. But this is fun information because I have always admired her wardrobe. Even though she can fill the Felt Forum for a religious seminar, she doesn't affect that pious I'm-too-spiritual-to-care-about-clothes attitude. She just wears short skirts and high heels and plenty of makeup.

Actually it's not entirely correct to call Mary Pat, New Age because she really is a proponent of Christian philosophy, but since that's hopelessly out of style, she frames everything within the teaching of her ancestors, who are Navajo Indians and Sunni Muslims.

"So what's suspicious about Mary Pat Johannsen?"

Poor Trip has to think some more about this. It is obvious that he has nothing to go on. He's just been trying to be polite after I have stuffed him with cavadells.

"Who's that big tall guy with the tattoo of a snake on his arm?" I ask, thinking of the guy from Le Jock, L.A.

"That's Snake. He works for Mr. Stallone."

"Doing what?"

"He manages the house. He's like....the butler."

I narrow my eyes and scowl, projecting a real testosterone-poisoned attitude. "He doesn't look like any house manager I've ever seen."

"Well, Mr. Stallone used to have one of those English butlers, but you know they can be a real pain in the ass. We used to call him the Prince Charles hand-me-down. But after he left Mr. Stallone hired Snake."

"What about the bald guy with the sack of pop-tops, the one who's always walking up and down the street looking for garbage?"

"Oh, that's Lucky. He lost everything in the real estate investment trust crash and Mr. Stallone feels sorry for him so lets him live in one of the gardener's cottages."

"None of this is any help, Trip."

"You could talk to that Mary Pat Johanssen yourself. I could work it out because she's coming to Mr. Stallone's party tonight."

I smother my excitement at this invitation with a serious law enforcement look. "Thanks Trip. That's a great idea. Have you ever considered a career in government? We could use a man like you."

Flattered, my friend Tripoli promises to think about it, and I send him off with several plastic containers of cavadells for his bodyguard friends. Later Trip brings the other bodyguards, Nick and Vinnie by to thank me. I invite them in to watch Oprah who's also doing a show today on steroid abuse, "Can it really really kill you?" This holds their rapt attention. I mean they don't even blink.

After serving up four espressos and then playing several hands of gin rummy with the guys during that difficult post-Oprah time of the day, I look out the window at Casa Stallone and wonder how much longer these guys are going to be here. Finally Trip pulls his bulk into a vertical position, studies the watch on his massive wrist, and announces that it's time to get ready for the party.

He leads me through a big electric gate and around to a side service door under a portico. Fortunately the rottweilers have been locked in their compound for the night. Trip takes me into the kitchen, where lots of people are preparing food. He tells me that we're going upstairs to the guest bedroom where I can change and fix my hair. I guess that's a hint.

It's on the way through the kitchen that I run directly into those two strange guys who not long ago chased me out of Le Jock, L.A. Trip introduces me to the tall guy with the tattoo, "Snake, I'd like you to meet ..."

I stick out my hand. "Molly Johnson, Don's little sister," I tell him. Trip looks at me kind of funny until I whisper in his ear, "Cover story."

Surprisingly Snake seems to believe this. However the little bald henchman Lucky is more suspicious. He looks at me then stares to his upper left, which any neuro-linguistic programmer will tell you is a sure sign he's searching to recover memory. I stand frozen like a deer fixed in the headlights of an eighteen wheeler.

"You look so familiar," he says slowly. "I know you."

"Maybe from another life," I suggest.

His leathery face crinkles into a grin while he tries to think. When I realize there's nothing in his memory bank for him to recover, I smile. The failure of both men to recognize me makes me wonder if the weight I've lost plus hacking off my hair in Bozeman, Montana, made a significant difference in my appearance, or if maybe they were just having a good Gallo day.

Trip takes me upstairs and turns me over to a beautiful six foot blonde telling me that she is Snake's girlfriend and her name is Lips, which I guess explains the significance of Snake's other bicep tattoo. Lips and Snake are a major mismatch. Lips can't be over twenty, and everything about her is lush, especially those big pouty lips. She's not just beautiful - she's the kind of gorgeous that screams out at you. Pairing her with Snake is like matching a young Kim Bassinger with a dim-witted Howard Stern. Although I have to admit that Lips herself does not appear to be a brain trust. She has an odd habit of sometimes focusing her eyes in the air just next to you. And she seems like if you told her something, she would fast forget it.

She also dresses like Snake in cutoff jeans and a leather vest that matches the one that Snake wears. Little lavender snake earrings dangle from her perfect ears, while a lavender streak waves through her otherwise blonde hair.

"The guys tell me I have to glitz you up." She motions to a giant marble Jacuzzi in the middle of the bathroom. "When you're done in the bath, you can pick out whatever you want to wear," and she opens the door to an enormous closet.

Not wanting to get naked in front of her, I tell Lips that I've just showered. She shrugs and heads for the Jacuzzi, shedding her clothing as she walks. This causes me to notice <u>her</u> tattoos: the butterfly on her right shoulder, the vine of roses on her ankle, and most ingenious of all, the two words tattooed on her buttocks. Read together from left to right they urge, "Do it!" I wonder what possible reason she could find to graffiti her lovely body, but this feeling is a reminder that I am old, old and hopelessly retro.

Idly, I flip through the clothes in the closet which are mostly gold lame, silver sequins, black chiffon - real girly stuff, and I just don't wear girly... even to a party. Margaret White, P.I., wouldn't wear this stuff and neither will I. Stubbornly, I sit down and cross my arms across my chest.

When Lips rises from her bubble bath (an intimidating sight) and pads out to the guest room, she eyes my negative body posture and adopts a rather commanding tone of voice. "Trip said that if you want to come to the party, you have to be dressed like everybody else."

I explain to her that I just don't dress that way...ever. But she calmly responds that I have no choice. So I pick out the least offensive thing, a black Aleia Azzedia and figure that's that, we're done with this make-over thing. But Lips starts right in on my hair. "It's got to be done," she insists with those petulant pouty lips.

"Forget it," I tell her.

"The cut is impossible," she complains and opens the door to a second closet which holds at least a dozen wigs on styrofoam heads. "Pick one out," she tells me.

Looking over the selection, I see that I can choose from the long strawberry shag of Ann Margaret, the dark bob of Demi Moore, or the tangled mane of Farah Fawcett. Yuck, I think, but since I have to make a decision I choose the platinum blonde thing that looks like it's been mixed with an egg beater. Basically tonight I'll be wearing Rod Stewart's hair.

Lips slips the wig on me, but I guess she's not satisfied with making me look like a Liverpudlian soccer groupie in drag. No, she's got to put some gunk on her fingertips and pull out the pieces of hair so I look like I'm being electrocuted.

To make matters worse, she insists on doing my makeup. I know I should try to stop her, but I've given up by now. If she makes me look like a raccoon, I'll just wipe it off later. When she gets done I look at myself in the mirror. And I am another woman, a magazine kind of woman - fake, funky.

And I look in the mirror from my perfectly modern face to the face of Mary Pat Johannsen who has just walked in. I turn to shake her hand. "Molly Johnson, Don's little sister," I tell her, and she gives me a warm hug as if we are old friends.

"I saw Don in Aspen in March," Mary Pat says. "We had a wonderful talk. The mountains are so conducive to the spiritual quest."

Apparently Mary Pat is also here for Lips to do her makeup. First though, Lips has to remove the makeup that Mary Pat has already put on, apparently for the purpose of walking across the street. Whatever! I'm thrilled. After all, this woman is the New Age Spiritual Giant, the Guru of the Decade who is packing them into Giant's Stadium, Wrigley Field, and the Houston Astrodome. Mary Pat looks at me closely, takes my hand, and then leans over to tell me what I presume to be a spiritual truth. "You look very nice," she says.

Wow! I feel as if I've gotten some kind of low level shock just from her touch. When I bring this to her attention, she tells me that this is a very common response, and she suspects that due to her increased spirituality, she may be reverberating on a higher electrical level than the rest of us.

I impose on Mary Pat by asking her to pray into my future. This is a combination of prayer and observing my karma for the purpose of prophesizing. I feel a little shoddy about this because the woman isn't working right now, she's just having her makeup done, but Mary Pat just beams as if nobody has ever asked her to do anything like that. And I can feel in myself a response of gratitude and a growing feeling that this really is an exceptional person whom I have had the amazing and intense good fortune to meet.

Mary Pat promises to do a future prayer as soon as Lips does her makeup. Even though Mary Pat is very unhappy with the foundation on the first go-round and gets a little crabby about it, the makeup job doesn't take too long, and Lips takes it all in stride. She gets that second coat of foundation just right, and soon Mary Pat is staring deep into my eyes and touching the tips of her fingers to mine.

Again there's an almost electric shock. Mary Pat seems to go off in a trance for a few minutes, emotions flickering across her face. These must be pleasant emotions because her facial antics most resemble the female face during orgasm. Of course I've only seen the female face during orgasm in movies, which are staged and produced by men, and the reliability of their perception is, I feel, questionable. When she's finished, Mary Pat reaches into her purse and I'm sure she's going to light up a cigarette, health risk or not. Instead she spritzes herself with a perfume spray and says "Everything's going to be fine."

"Fine how? Fine in exactly what way?" I ask.

"All your dreams will come true."

I laugh. "Isn't that an ancient Chinese curse?"

Mary Pat applies an extra coat of mascara. "Yes, but you're not Chinese, so for you it's not a curse." She smooths the skirt of her purple silk suit, sucks in her stomach, and heads for the door. "Oh, by the way," she tells me pausing at the threshold, "if you experience any telephathic experiences or extrasensory perception, don't be alarmed. Many people have that for a few days after touching me."

Mary Pat leaves and Lips motions me toward the open door. "Wish me luck," I say to Lips who I'm sure has no idea what I'm talking about nor any interest either.

"Good luck," she whispers anyway.

Chapter Twelve

I walk down a grand circular staircase into a marble foyer full of palm trees and glittering lights. I don't know if the massive palms were moved inside just for the party or if they live there all the time, but they sure look good.

At the bottom of the stairs, he stands. Wearing black silk Gianni Versace, Sylvester balances a silver tray holding a dozen flutes of bubbly. Sylvester Stallone...serving drinks at his own party! It's just so unaffected and homey and Martha Stewart, I have trouble absorbing the image.

"Champagne?" he asks in that voice I know so well.

As I reach for a glass I take a good look at him. Up close he looks older than I expected however I remind myself that my Stallone obsession has been based on the twenty-five year old Stallone. In front of me is not an obsession or a dream, but a real person.

So I concentrate and try to take a good clean fresh look. I see a man who is tanned, fit, and cordial. I see an Italianate face, a slightly crooked mouth and the animal magnetism that comes with great wealth. But I begin to realize that I'd better worry about what Stallone sees when he looks at me rather than the other way around. Fortunately there is no glimmer of recognition in his eyes, so I guess I have escaped detection as the crazy woman in the gym.

Before I can think of anything to say, Sylvester moves off to offer champagne to the other guests. When I realize Lips is standing next to me, I squeeze her arm nervously. She steers me into a huge room dominated by a three-story teardrop Waterford crystal chandelier that sparkles in the light like the Cartier diamonds.

I look around at the crowd. Everybody is dressed in black, and everybody has messy hair. So even though I think I look bizarre, I actually look just like everybody else, except for May Pat Johannsen, who has normal hair and is dressed in purple. "Who are these people?" I ask Lips.

"Except for the industry people and Sly's kids and ex-wives, this crowd is mostly New York publishing people because this is a party for Sly's new book. It's his analysis of the sixteenth century Flemish painters. He wanted to do something nice for everybody who worked on the book, so he flew them in for the party."

"I didn't know he was an art expert."

"Oh, he's very smart and always reading," she tells me.

Gee, I was expecting him to be shrewd but I certainly wasn't expecting him to be an intellectual. From across the room, a tall bony woman swoops down on us. She wears a severe black sheath with a scoop neckline that exposes her prominent collarbones and scrawny neck. A cap of black hair surrounds her face which is all straight lines and angles, and she has that wide eyed perpetual stare that is most often the result of a bad face lift.

"Isn't Sly out of this world?" the woman gushes. "I mean, he must have problems. Everyone has problems. But Sylvester has somehow transcended to a different mental and spiritual plane than the rest of us."

"Well, he's a guy who lives life," I mutter.

"Oh, I like that. He's a guy who lives life," she repeats. "Is that yours or somebody else's?" fixing me with her cat-like surgical stare.

"Well, if it wasn't mine, I would have attributed it to the author."

Lips elbows me hard in the side, but it never occurs to me that she is trying to warn me. The stick woman takes my arm, "I'm always interested in fresh ideas. Let's go over in that corner."

Despite the fact that Lips is rolling her eyes at me, I talk with this strange woman for quite a while, expounding on my favorite topics; life, courage, and womanhood, during which time, Lips tries to get my attention. Finally I interrupt my monologue just to go over to Lips and ask her to please stop distracting me. In return she grabs my arm. "That's Wendy Kroy!"

"So?"

"She's a producer...sort of...she develops ideas."

"And?" I'm really not seeing the problem here.

Lips gives me a look like I'm incredibly dense, "Look I don't know where you're from or what's your gig but Wendy's speciality is ideas- as in, other people's ideas. None of the creative people will talk to her because she's like a giant sponge. She'll suck up whatever is new and innovative about your thinking and then get somebody else to write it up for union minimum. You wouldn't believe the stories about the things she's done. I don't even know how she got in here. She wasn't invited. She must have crashed."

But we don't have time to get any further with this because Wendy slides back over to us. "Oh is this girl talk, let me in on this."

Sylvester whispers in the ear of the tuxedoed pianist at the white baby grand piano near the french doors. And I notice that what follows is a little "American in Paris" followed by a skillful and subtle rendition of Cole Porter, then Vivaldi's Spring from the "The Four Seasons", and finally a little Billy Joel "Piano Man." It is at this point that incredibly Sylvester walks over to us. My heart is pounding like I have the lead in the high school play.

"Are you having a good time?" he asks.

I open my mouth, but nothing comes out.

"I hear the Big Apple is having a cold snap. Twenty-four degrees. But what do we care, right?"

Here he is - Sylvester Stallone standing right in front of me - center of my dream, however crazed and obsessed and irrational - the reason for my trans-continental journey, the object of my quest, whatever the hell it is. So why don't I answer him? Where's my nerve when I need it?

Wendy Kroy takes maximum advantage of this conversational lull, taking Sylvester by the arm, "You know, Sly, I've always seen you as a man who 'Lives life.' That's the phrase I immediately associate with you. "He lives life." Now I think there are some great marketing spin-offs from that. Let's go out by the pool."

I slug down my champagne, disgusted with myself. How many chances do I think I'm going to get? Lips looks at me and shakes her head. "If you want to talk to him, you should just do it."

I follow Sly and Wendy out by the pool, but everywhere Sylvester goes a little crowd immediately forms around him and I cannot seem to break through it. When he slips away from Wendy and heads into the kitchen, I follow. The kitchen is restaurant sized with big stoves and giant aluminum and glass refrigerators. Snake, dressed in a tuxedo (an enormous visual contradiction) is picking up a fresh tray of canapes from the counter. "These people are so pushy," he complains to Sylvester. "They're stepping all over each other to grab the hors d'oeuvres. It's not like they're hungry. They just want to be first."

Sylvester pats him on his bony shoulder. "They can't help it. It's the effect of the constant cold and hustle on their personalities. Just be patient and smile, they'll settle down." In a flash Sylvester is out of the kitchen again. I try for the next forty minutes to catch up with him or break through the little cluster always surrounding him but I have no luck.

So when I see <u>The Decline and Fall of the Roman Empire</u> by Gibbons on the table next to the Eames recliner, I decide to take a break. A little Gibbons always calms my nerves. I sit down, slip my shoes, and curl up with the book. As I read, I'm bothered by the itchy wig and try to scratch my head without disturbing the wig. That's when I see Sly peering at me curiously. "You like that book?" he asks.

"Sure... it's the best on degenerating Rome, although Will and Ariel Durant didn't do a bad job."

"That book has been on that table for two years and you're the first person to pick it up."

"Really?"

"Let's get some fresh air."

Chapter Thirteen

We walk out the front door and down the long driveway and out the gate. "Don't go near the van," he tells me. "I've got a temporary problem with a stalker. She says she's from the BATF, but I don't believe it."

"That's terrible," I say and we walk the other way.

"So what's your story?" he asks. "Why are you the first person to come to my party and read Gibbons?" I don't know what to say to that. But while I'm thinking, Sylvester interrupts. "Is it because 'Reading is to the mind, what exercise is to the body?' Richard Steele, 1989."

Whoa! I think. Is he really quoting Richard Steele at me? This is my kind of fun. Having been schooled in Minimalism, I reach into my bag of handy Hemingway quotes. "'Then it would sound as though I were claiming an erudition I do not possess.' Ernest Hemingway, 1939." We both laugh and this changes Sylvester's entire face. I feel so comfortable with him, like we're old friends.

"I think you're a writer," he accuses me cheerfully.

"Well,..."

"Only writers talk like that." Sylvester falls into step beside me as we walk down Eldorado Boulevard which is deserted except for security personnel and the video monitors that swivel as we walk past. "I should have guessed," Sylvester says. "I'm always sympatico with writers."

"Why is that?"

"Probably because I started out as a writer. But let's talk about you. Tell me why you're working for a publishing house instead of writing?"

I take a deep breath and explain that I'm not working for a publishing house and that I have written a book and I start telling him about my novel and short stories. I talk way past the point of polite, but he seems interested.

"I agree with you," he says when I finally take a breath. "I like the Margaret White idea better than the short stories."

I look him over and he seems sincere.

"Mostly because I'd love to see a really great woman detective," he says.

I sigh. I've heard men say this before and I've never met one who really meant it. What they really mean is that they don't want the feminist argument that will ensue when they admit that for action dramas they really want a male hero. My skepticism must show on my face because Sylvester says, "You don't believe me."

I hesitate,..."Well, let's just say it's unusual."

"Why don't you give me a copy of the manuscript, stay overnight and we'll discuss it in the morning."

"Stay over tonight?" I manage.

"Sure. You can stay in one of the guesthouses. I'll see you at nine by the pool?"

I don't answer right away, I'm stunned. He leans over and touches my arm. "Okay?"

A brilliant Beverly Hills morning is a nice thing to wake up to. Light that is a completely different color from any morning light I have ever known enters my coral silk bedroom. The little ormolu clock formerly owned by Jacqueline Kennedy Onassis reads 6:00 A.M., which surprises me because I never wake up at six o'clock, at least not voluntarily.

But I prowl about, find a coffeemaker and some chocolate raspberry coffee, which enables me to lounge about drinking Sylvester's gourmet coffee and enjoying his view. There's a lovely English garden close to the house, well planted and lined with curving walkways. I'd love to take a walk outside and sit on the pretty stone bench, but I can see through the double windows that the rottweilers are out and about.

Since I can find nothing better to do and I'm nervous, I work out on the Nordic track and the Stairmaster located in the giant marble bathroom. Then I shower and feed the hamsters which I brought in from the van last night when I gave my Margaret White, P.I. manuscript to Trip to deliver to Sylvester.

I also took advantage of this opportunity to explain to Trip that even though I work for the BATF (confidentially), I am also Don Johnson's little sister Molly, and that I am a writer and my pen name is Molly Malone and that's how I would like to be addressed in the future. Naturally I explain to him that all this is an extremely big secret and remind him to keep a suspicious eye on the neighbors. I figure that should take care of straightening out my stories - unless Don Johnson comes to visit.

Looking at the clock I can see that it's getting close to nine, and I'd better get dressed. Even though our meeting will be a working session. Still this is Beverly Hills and we are meeting poolside, so I do wonder what I should wear.

Several bathing suits hang from hooks in the big bathroom but there's not a chance in hell that I am going to put on one of them. Instead I dress in my uniform; Black jeans, a man's white undershirt, sleeves rolled up, and my red cowboy boots. Looking at myself in the mirror, I decide that the only thing missing from my ensemble is a pack of cigarettes rolled up in the folds of my t-shirt sleeves. I am that close to James Dean.

There's nobody at the pool when I go out. However, the trainers have begun running the rottweilers through their attack and slash routines so I know at least that the dogs are under control and I don't have to worry about them practising on me.

It's 9:03 on my watch and nobody is around except for the help: the aerobics instructors, the bodyguards, the dog trainers, the gardeners. Eventually Sylvester comes out of the main house wearing a Gianni Versace black silk bathing suit and carrying a black velvet towel. He walks over to me and hands me the towel. Then he walks over to the diving board and makes a perfect jack knife dive into the pool.

When he swims across the pool and emerges dripping, the L.A. sun is so bright behind Sylvester that the edges of him radiate light. After rubbing himself vigorously with the black towel, Sylvester settles in next to me on one of the teakwood chaises with English chintz cushions. I try not to notice his bronzed and bulging muscles; the triceps, the biceps, the well cut washboard stomach.

When Snake appears with a tray holding two chilled wineglasses filled with orange juice, I take the first one, Sylvester the second, and Snake slithers away. "Where'd you ever find him?" I ask, referring to Snake.

"I stole him from Frank Sinatra."

"Get outta here."

"Some people don't like Snake because he's a little different, but he's loyal and most of my favorite people are a little different."

I know what he means because that always happens to me too.

"But Molly," Sly now puts his hand on my shoulder. "Let's not prolong this because I have to tell you, I love your book."

"You do?"

"Absolutely. It's bright. It's wild and clever. You created a real action hero in female form. It's an amazing piece of work."

"What did you think of the opening?" I ask. I've been a little worried that the opening is slow even though I discussed this with several truckers while driving cross-country, and they thought it was okay.

"Well, I guess I agree with John Updike when he said, 'When I write I aim in my mind not toward New York but toward a vague spot a little to the east of Kansas.'"

I take a sip of orange juice and think that one over.

"I do, however, see one major problem with the concept," Sylvester tells me.

Oh dear I knew things were going too well. Bracing myself I ask, "What's that?"

"Your time period."

"I don't understand."

"If you place Margaret White, Private Investigator, in the frame of present time, everybody is going to jump on you for being politically incorrect. You're going to have critics arguing that Margaret shouldn't drop-kick the vegetarian bisexual handicapped animal rights activist even if she is the murderer because it sends a negative message on animal rights, on vegetables, on bisexuality, and on handicapped activists."

"I see what you mean. But I don't see how I can do Margaret honestly and still satisfy the critics in terms of political correctness."

"I think you have to rewrite your story in the future or in the past."

That's not a bad idea. In fact as I think back I realize that I always had a nervous feeling whenever I got Margaret into a confrontation with some sacred cow, probably because I was subconsciously projecting the massive political panning that Sylvester has suggested. "You know, it does solve a lot of problems."

I turn his suggestion over in my mind. "But if I set it in the future," I say thinking out loud, "then I'm doing science fiction, which has never been my bag."

"I think the past is a better idea anyway and I have a suggestion."

"Which is what?"

"As a metaphor for our times, I would propose a setting of degenerating Rome."

"Hmm, I really know that period."

"It's a wonderful dramatic setting. There's a great schism between the wealthy powerful class and the impoverished horde and there's lots of action. There's the Colosseum, the gladiators, the degeneration of the nobility, the uprising of the Barbarian horde."

"Mmm, lots of action," I admit, but I'm not sure I can have a Margaret White heroine in Ancient Rome. I mean we're talking heavy patriarchy here. We're talking a time period when the family patriarch owns the wife and children like cows or sheep. "I don't think I can put a functioning woman detective into that kind of patriarchial setting."

"It's a creative problem," Sylvester concedes. "Let's go for a drive. But first we have to pick up Arnold."

Chapter Fourteen

Arnold Schwarzenegger lives in a huge white mansion with marble Doric columns and a reflecting pool in front. Next to this Goliath of a house is another residence, surrounded by trucks and cement mixers. Sylvester explains to me that this will be the site of Arnold's new think tank. This takes a moment to sink in. Arnold Schwarzenegger ... think tank?

"Arnold has hired the greatest minds from an eclectic group of sciences and pseudo-sciences, including not only world-recognized economists and nuclear engineers but also psychics, policemen, artists, and athletes.

At Schwarzenegger's, I expect to be met by a servant or bodyguard, but Arnold himself comes out onto an upstairs balcony to greet us. He has his little children with him and looks every bit the Daddy. "Sylvester, you Napleanic cur," he calls from the balcony. "Get up here and say hello to the kids."

Sly and I make our way past the architects carrying plans for the think-tank past Maria who is hard at work conducting an at-home satellite interview with the contenders for control of the Russian empire. Still she's not too busy to smile that dazzling Kennedy-Shriver smile at us as we go up to the balcony.

When I see Arnold up close, I am temporarily overwhelmed by his dimensions. The massive body, the slightly gap-toothed smile, the curious affectation of the big Winston Churchill cigar all combine to create the gut level sense that he is the most powerful man in the world. Oh sure, there are men who have more money, and there are men with better political connections. But in terms of personal power, in terms of a strong charismatic feeling of rightness and safety, Arnold is the man.

He sits with one child on each massive leg. Arnold explains that he is telling them a story from his hometown in Austria. They listen intently to the heavily accented tale. I listen too and am surprised how striking a resemblance it bears to the "Itsy Bitsy Spider."

When Arnold has finished and the kids are off for their language lessons, he slaps Sylvester on the back. "And how is the Italian this morning? Is he happy or is he sad?" Arnold looks at me and winks, "We Austrians are only right minded and industrious."

Sylvester rolls his eyes at what is obviously an ongoing joke. "Arnold, I'd like you to meet a friend of mine, Molly Malone."

Arnold turns his hazel eyes on me. Never have I been so microscopically scrutinized. I feel under his intense inspection that he can not only see right through me, but he can also lift off layers like clear laminate over an anatomy model. He smiles and the grin is wide. "She's not from California," he tells Sylvester.

"No."

Arnold looks at me again, a gaze no less piercing and intrusive than the first. "Is she all right?" he asks Sylvester.

"Absolutely."

"Then I like her," Arnold announces, looking at me with a mixture of friendship and respect. I know that I haven't done anything to earn his friendship, so it must come either from Sylvester's recommendation or else from some sort of intuition that accompanied Arnold's study of my facial features. Still it seems steadfastly reliable. As I smile back at Arnold I feel somehow that the three of us together are something special.

"Okay, down to business," Arnold says. "Whose car? Yours or mine?"

"Have you hired a driver yet?"

"Sly, Sly, you know I am a man of the people. You know I don't approve of those bourgeois insulating trappings of wealth."

Sylvester points to what looks to me like a small armored vehicle from one of Arnold's movies. Although it looks too small for Arnold, it does seem to be the perfect urban vehicle. "He drives himself in that ridiculous Humvee. Let's take my car," Sylvester suggests.

Arnold smiles his big gap-toothed grin. "I'm easy. Besides the Humvee wouldn't start this morning."

We head down the massive circular staircase, wave at Maria and step outside. Nick and Vinnie and Trip wait in the stretch limo, their big sausage arms pressed against each other in the back seat.

"Do we really need the bodyguards, Sly? After all, we do have Molly." Arnold apparently cannot pass up an opportunity to rib Sylvester.

"The bodyguards needed to get out," I explain to Arnold. "They've been sitting around the house too long, and we don't want them to get rusty."

Familiar with the psychology of security, Arnold acquiesces. "Allright, allright," he says, as we slide into the seats in front of Sly's bodyguards. "But I control the music."

"I'm not up for classical right now," Sylvester tells him. "I'm in the mood for country western."

"No, no, no." Arnold insists. "We listen to country western when we visit the Planet Hollywood in Aspen. We listen to rap and heavy metal when we visit the restaurant in New York. Here in L.A. we listen to classical. I'll give you a choice: Schumann or Bach?"

"Which Bach?"

"Anna Magdalena Bach. I always favor the ladies, you know. Ask Maria."

"Okay, okay, Bach."

Arnold smiles his big healthy Germanic grin. "I like to have my own way you know," he says. Then he tells Snake, who has just gotten behind the wheel, "Give Molly the tour - the whole enchilada."

I raise my tinted window, not shutting out the real world but giving me just the clearest, nicest air-conditioned view of it. Sitting between the two muscular moguls in the middle section of the big white limo, I am aware than I am surrounded by hundreds of pounds of muscle. While Arnold does not flaunt his muscles under silk as Sylvester does, aiming for a more bank-chairman-playing-tennis image, still I am aware of his beefy biceps on my left, just as I feel Sylvester's on my right. And this is a very pleasant feeling. Another woman might feel intimidated or tongue-tied, but I feel as if I have found my perfect place in the universe, my sweet spot. "Okay what's the plan?" I ask.

Arnold lights up the big Winston Churchill cigar and gestures with his huge hands. "The plan is to marshal the great brains of every science to solve the really important problems. Nuclear fusion is first of course but there are so many others; world hunger, disease, war, environmental deterioration, religious disputes, intolerance, racism, sexism..."

I interrupt him, "I mean, where are we going?"

"We'll know when we get there," Sly answers mysteriously and Snake winds us through Malibu, past Grauman's Chinese Theatre, slides us by the La Brea Tar pits, slithers us along the precipitous cliffs of Topanga Canyon, then past the skating paths of Venice Beach. To me, the motion and the silence are wonderful for I find myself in a creative stew, a bubbling pot of thoughts that will surely lead to the new vision that puts the perfect angle on Sly's suggestion of rewriting Margaret White, P.I. in the time period of Ancient Rome.

Snake parks on Rodeo Drive while Sly, Arnold, and I, surrounded by our meaty friends Trip, Vinnie, and Nick, try to shop. Unfortunately, we do have to put up with Arnold's constant proclamations about the silliness of the expensive merchandise, but I am starting to get used to him and find I can just shop right through it. Orange leather jodphurs cost $8,500 on Rodeo Drive and I am studying the french seams in a plain white blouse for $4,500 when Sly becomes insistent about buying something for me.

Actually he wants to buy lots of stuff for me. Maybe he always does that when he goes shopping with someone. But I certainly don't want him spending money on me. Unfortunately however, I can see that he is getting very uncomfortable with my refusals. And even though I have only known Sylvester for a short time, I feel very close to him and I want to deal with his eccentric insistence on buying something for me in a tactful manner. So when we pass a jewelry shop that has an excruciatingly simple Knot of Hercules on a gold chain, I allow him to purchase it for me, on the condition that he buy two additional gold knots -- one for Arnold, and one for himself. The golden Knot of Hercules, the ancient expression of the bond of friendship, will be a memento of our day and a symbol of our growing friendship. As we fasten the gold necklaces around our necks, I look from one face to the another and project a future of late night adventures and harrowing escapes from dangerous drinking establishments in exotic locales.

But Sly wants a cappuccino so we take a break from shopping and slip into a charming little alfresco cafe where the palm fronds brush the sides of the ebony marble tables. I realize that this is the perfect time for me to share the thoughts that have been running through my mind since we had our long limo drive. First, of course, I have to bring Arnold up to speed on the fact that I'm writing a book with a female action hero and he asorbs this very quickly.

"Okay, guys - picture this - we take the lead character, Margaret White, back in time to the age of the Amazon culture so she can be an Amazon detective and we have her solve a case related to the disintegration of the Roman Empire."

Sylvester rubs his chin, "Interesting. The Amazon legend of the woman warrior ...hmm." Arnold relights his cigar while Sylvester thinks. "Of course there is a time problem, because the first scientific evidence of Amazon activity dates back to 300 B.C. while the actual disintegration of the Roman Empire was around 400 A.D."

I nod because I know he's referring to the gravesites of the first female warriors found in Soviet Georgia and I do have to admit that 300 B.C. to 400A.D. is a time glitch, but I don't see it as a major problem. "But what if the heroine is a member of a small Amazon tribe that has survived in isolation for seven centuries," I propose. "And while our heroine is hunting with her sisters, she is kidnapped by a band of slavers, who take her to Rome where she is sold in the marketplace. However..." I take a breath, "our heroine saves the life of her master thereby earning her freedom, and after that she functions as a free agent in Rome and makes her living as a bodyguard and detective.

"Well," Sly rubs his jaw. "I do like the concept of an Amazon detective sleuthing around Ancient Rome."

"I don't know," Arnold hesitates. "I think you will have to change her name...?"

"How about Marga? We'll call her Marga?"

And this is where we are - me and Sly and Arnold, laughing in the sunlight at our little alfresco table when without warning, a long dark shadow blocks our light.

Chapter Fifteen

The shadow belongs to the tall woman at the next table who has just stood up and turned around. Wearing a dark brown dress, her black hair hidden by a wide brimmed hat with a linen band the color of red earth and a thick prickly necklace that seems to be made of sticks, it takes me a moment to recognize Wendy Kroy. "Sly! Arnold! What luck," she gushes, "I was just going to call you."

Both Sly and Arnold stand up and begin backing out.

"I was going to schedule an appointment, but this is just too synchronicitous. So we have to talk right now because I have the greatest idea."

"We've changed our office procedures, Wendy," Sly tells her. "I don't listen to any proposals unless my office manager's already passed on them."

"Me, too," Arnold says quickly. Meanwhile Arnold and Sly are skillfully backing out of the narrow alcove, which leaves me alone at the table, a sitting duck so to speak. Wendy seeing the inevitability of their retreat, swivels around, positions herself directly in front of me and snorts, "Hmmmph, nobody has any manners anymore." Then she slides into the empty chair next to me, "So you really had them going with that Amazon thing.

Uh-oh, she's obviously overheard me. "I didn't say Amazons, I said Alaskans."

"Bullshit!" she pulls out a lipstick that's the same muddy color as her jewelry and she applies it carefully, "What did you say your name was?"

"Molly Johnson."

Wendy laughs, "Oh yeah, Don's little sister. That's cute." She leans her face in close to mine and her breath smells like mold and must and rotting melon. "Let me explain the protocol around here. Like most animal activities, we have turf and we have a food chain. I've been working here for the past fourteen years and I've staked out a career in developing action films, well lately action/adventure. But you have no turf and you're very low on the food chain, so you have only two choices. You can work <u>for</u> me..." She hands me her business card. "Or I'll have to eat you up."

That's when I realize that Sly and Arnold have left me with the check. So I'm standing up reaching into my pocket to pay, hoping Wendy didn't hear my whole darn story premise when I'm interrupted by a woman trailing a ten-year-old boy. "Can you direct me to the ice rink?" she asks.

"The ice rink?" I cannot believe she said this to me. I mean what made her think that I was a woman who would know the location of the ice rink? Then impulsively I do a stupid thing. Nodding toward the boy I ask, "Is he in the house league or the competitive league?"

Naurally she is delighted at my question. "Competitive team, Burbank, Squirt level. We just drove in for the game."

Then I tell her that I have four boys in competitive hockey in Maine and actually say what a wonderful hockey program we have. I can't believe I am doing this. It's like one of those near-death experiences where I've risen out of my body and look down on my other self who speaks at machine-gun speed and with combustible enthusiasm to this hockey mother on topics from the importance of the length of the radius of the skate blade to the percentage of junior league players who receive college scholarships.

Eventually the woman walks away from me to ask someone else where the ice rink is. After paying the check, I walk back to the limo shaking my head. It must have been Wendy's threat that so unnerved me, that I had this lapse (The kind of thing that happens to alcoholics and food abusers) and although I must forgive myself this temporary slip, I do think it's a very bad sign.

When we get back to the limo Sly announces with a sort of urgency that he has to 'work out' and Arnold nods in somber agreement. Then Sly looks at Arnold and says "Let's take Molly over to Wicked Eric." Since I'm a woman who's been a good wife and mother for a very long time, the idea of meeting someone named Wicked Eric, is intriguing to say the least.

Snake drives through Brentwood while Arnold begins a rather didactic monologue on how every person has an obligation to keep his body physically fit. Sly arranges his face into an expression of utmost seriousness and agrees with him. I wonder if they're trying to tell me something. When Snake drives us up a little knoll to the locked gate of a brick mini-mansion, Sly speaks into the security intercom set in brick columns, the gate opens, and Snake drives in and parks.

The body guards get out and stretch (those densely packed big beefy muscles tighten up fast) but Sly and Arnold and I walk into the big open garage which houses several black limosines as well as a few sports cars. "Who's house is this?" I ask Arnold.

"It belongs to the guy who owns the limo company but we're looking for Wicked Eric."

We find Eric in his little studio apartment which is actually a partitioned part of garage Eric shares with a red Lamborghini. When Arnold calls me over for the introduction, I realize that he's called Wicked Eric because he's so wicked handsome. Thick dark hair, light blue eyes, straight nose, and perfect jaw, Eric has the face of a rugged male model, complemented by broad shoulders that taper down to a small waist, nice buns, and long cowboy legs. "We want you to take over Molly," Sly tells him.

Eric gives Sly a steely glance. "I don't do broads."

Arnold frowns, "She's not a broad."

"She looks like a broad," Eric eyes me up and down.

Arnold loses the frown and turns cajoling. "Look Eric we know you've never done women and we understand that your special skill is in the aesthetics of muscular proportions, while women are culturally judged by ...."

"the proportions of their fat deposits." Sly adds.

"But we want you to make a special exception for Molly," Arnold continues.

"Why?"

Sly puts his arm around me. "She's our friend."

"She's a chick." Eric may be wicked handsome but he's not making a great first impression on me.

"You owe me Eric," Sly reminds him. "I've given you alot of training jobs with people in the industry. I've given you driving work."

I interrupt at this point. "Driving work?"

"Eric is a a part-time physical trainer and a part-time limo driver." Arnold tells me. "... a Renaissance man."

Yeah, I know what that means. It means Eric can't make enough of a living at either one of the two and so he lives in the garage of the house that belongs to his boss.

Eric gives me the quick little smile of a man with no alternatives, "Has she got any musculature at all. I'd like a look."

I frown at Sly, "What's he talking about?"

"He wants to see you in your underwear in order to estimate your muscle to fat ratio."

"Forget about it."

Eric looks to Sly and Arnold for support and finding none, he sighs with exaggerated frustration. "You can't expect me to take this job and work with whatever is under there," Eric points his finger at me and my baggy clothes.

"That's exactly what we expect," they tell him.

Eric paces up and down for a while before giving in, "All right, all right. But this is a special favor because as you know beefing up broads is not my line of work."

This statement makes me feel like a piece of veal, which is a meat I don't even eat in sympathy for the confinement of the baby cows. And you know since we got here, no one has even asked my opinion. Has anybody considered that maybe I don't want to weight train? I think about pointing this out to them. But both Sly and Arnold have been so incredibly sweet to me and I really do want to fit in and be one of the guys, so I keep quiet. Meanwhile Sly has taken out a notebook, "So what do you want her to start on?"

Eric begins talking about chromium supplements and kelp, branched chain amino acid protein powders and anabolic accelerators. When he finishes his litany of chemicals, Eric strides over to me and pulling up the short sleeve of my tee shirt, he gives my almost non existent right bicep a squeeze. "If I wanted to I could turn you into a work of art," he says in an odd tone of voice, and I think as I pull away from him that there is something not quite right about Wicked Eric.

When we finally get back to the estate, Sly and Arnold and I while away the rest of the day with a candlelit dinner by the pool followed by a game of cards in the recreational wing of the mansion. We'd like to have a fourth, but the guys will only consider Bruce Willis and he's out of town.

Before I realize it, it's late and I'm back in my guest house. The ormolu clock reads 11:00 P.M. but I'm so full of excitement I wonder how I'm ever going to fall asleep. I keep reviewing the events of the day like rewinding a tape. Yes, they like me. Yes, they like my story. And they even want me to weight train. Somehow that seems to be the ultimate compliment.

As I stare at the little clock, I realize that back in Bangor, Maine, it's now 8:00 which is the perfect time to call home - if I was stupid enough to do such a thing. There is a phone on the desk. I look at it ...and then I pick it up. And when my hand touches the phone, the oddest thing happens. I can see Dash. I can actually see him! He's in the recreation room playing cards with Mitch and two other hockey fathers; Don Kirnan and Paul Maglione. The vision is as clear as if I were there. This startles me so much that I involuntarily jump a little, causing my hand to leave the phone.

When my hand leaves the phone, the vision disappears so I put my hand back on the phone. Again I see Dash with his friends playing cards and drinking beer. They have the big 48-inch T.V. tuned in to a hockey game. And through the half-glass wall of the recreation room I can see all the boys skating on the covered rink that Dash built in our backyard.

I decide that I must be having some kind of hallucination due to my physical contact with Mary Pat Johannsen the evening before. Whatever the reason, I do keep my hand on the phone because I want to see what happens.

Paul gets up from the card table, walks over to the glass, and looks out at the ice. "What a cold snap! What do you think the temperature is out there, Dash?"

"I don't know." Dash doesn't look up from his cards.

Paul bites his lower lip. "I can't bring Jeremy home with frostbite again."

"That's right, the Moms don't like it when their little boys' faces are three different colors," Don adds.

"I say it's time for another round." Dash gets up and goes to the refrigerator.

Mitchell follows him over. "So what's your mother really doing here?" he asks, speaking low so the others don't hear.

Dash shrugs. "She likes to come over now and then. She likes to clean and iron. All that shit."

"So where's Molly?"

"I told you. She went on a little shopping trip."

Mitch shakes his head. "I told that to Barb. She didn't buy it. She said that Molly would never take a major shopping trip without her. She thinks you killed Molly. She keeps looking out the kitchen window into your yard. She think's you're going to come out some night and bury her."

Dash looks really annoyed. "How could I bury her in the backyard? The ground's still frozen."

"That's what I told Barb. But she keeps bugging me. I've got to tell her something else pretty soon, or she's gonna make trouble."

"Geeze, Mitch, just because your wife is wearing your jockey shorts, does this mean I can't have a life over here?"

"Did you have a fight? Can I tell her that? Maybe she'd believe it and leave me alone."

"If you tell her that Mitch she'll tell every goddamn person she meets. The official line is that Molly went shopping. I expect you, as my friend, to hold to that official line."

"Okay, okay." Mitch pops the top on a Coors and looks around. "What's it like around here with the four boys and your mother in the house?"

Dash gives him a nasty look. "It's terrific."

Mitch delivers a six-pack of cold Coors to the card table, and Paul and Don leave the window and head for the beer. "Don't you think the boys have had enough?" Don asks.

"You can't make the NHL if you're afraid of the cold," Dash answers. "Let's play poker."

I really don't understand how I can see directly into my home. Is it telepathy or ESP? Is the information traveling through the air or over the phone lines? I don't know and I don't care. I'm having too good a time. I decide to add to the fun by dialing my home number.

Dash's mother answers. She's up in the kitchen, making homemade spaghetti sauce. "Allo, Denton residence." Dash's mother always does that fake French stuff. I hate it. I don't see how marrying a French Canadian should give a French accent to an Italian.

"Hi. Is Dash home?"

"Molleee cherie, how are you?"

I mutter something appropriate. Nobody really listens to how you respond to that question anyway.

"Dash is very busy, but I will go and get him." My mother-in-law is such a sport. I watch her walk to the back of the house and call "Dash, you have a phone call."

"I'm playing cards," Dash answers brusquely.

Maria ambles back to the kitchen phone. "He can't come to the phone right now," she tells me sweetly.

"Tell him it's me."

"I did, honey."

"No, you didn't. Walk back down the hall and tell him that it's me on the phone." Maria makes a funny face, but she does it.

Dash gets up quickly and hurries up the stairs. "I'll take it in the bedroom," he tells his mother. Dash rushes upstairs to our bedroom. He heads for the phone, but then stops for a moment. He takes a breath or two and composes himself. Slowly he sits on the bed. Slowly he picks up the receiver. "Yes?" he says coldly.

Chapter Sixteen

"Hi, Dash."

"Who is this?" he demands as if he doesn't know.

"You sound out of breath."

"Where the hell are you, Molly?"

"Promise you won't get mad?"

Dash smashes his fist into the wall, grimaces, and then replaces the receiver against his ear. "What am I supposed to tell our sons, Molly?"

"Tell them whatever you want. I didn't plan this, you know. It was more of a spur of the moment thing."

"Oh well, I guess that makes it all okay. So where the hell are you?"

"Are you calm, Dash?"

"Of course I'm calm."

It is such fun to watch Dash seethe with fury. I take a deep breath and focus on really enjoying the moment. "I'm spending the night at the home of Sylvester Stallone."

Dash sighs. Then he shields his brow with his hand as if he's protecting himself from scorching heat. "Molly, if you're in trouble, if you're on drugs or something, just say so. I'll help you."

He is such a riot, I have to laugh. Unfortunately this makes him mad. "If you have something to say to me, you'd better say it fast because I'm hanging up," he snarls.

"I'm staying in the guest house of the Stallone estate in Beverly Hills, California - on business. I just thought I'd call so you wouldn't think I'd been kidnapped or something."

"That's what you want to say to me. You're telling me that you're actually going to continue this" -- he searches for the right word -- "insult."

"Geez, Dash, this is the chance of a lifetime."

"Fine. I don't know what you're talking about or why you've done this but everything comes with a price and you're gonna have to pay for this, Molly...bigtime. Oh, by the way, you lost your teaching job."

Dash actually hangs up the phone on me. I watch him take several deep breaths to calm himself before walking out of the bedroom and down the stairs.

His mother is in the kitchen, stirring the sauce. "So is Molly tired of buying clothes yet? She sounded kind of cranky."

Dash clenches and unclenches his fists. "She's great. Everything is just great."

After the vision I feel ... very relaxed, like I've had a good long soak in a hot tub. I fall asleep easily and sleep so well that I don't wake up for almost two days. Jet lag - who knows?. But when Lips finally wakes me up, the guys are ready for another adventure. And we spend the night club crawling through all the trendy celebrity-owned nightclubs of Sly and Arnold's friends.

Jack Nicholson's Monkey Bar is decorated like an African jungle. Grease is a fifties place with biker chic and Nerds and Oliva Newton-John lookalikes. OUT is full of drag queens, nose rings, and lots of other interesting pierced body parts. There's a place called Siamese where you can't get in unless you're bound to your partner ala Siamese twins. But we don't stay there too long because Sly and I don't like the way the doorman has duct taped our ankles together.

Halfway through the evening I realize that I've completely lost my ability to be shocked at humanity in any form or condition. I have also become very comfortable with faux: Faux dungeons, faux motorcycles, faux harems, faux butcher shops, faux corrals, faux oases.

I also notice something else - there's something sparking between Sly and me. There's been a certain amount of lingering eye contact. I'm sure he started it, but I must admit I've done my share. We've been dancing and mutual body awareness is so heightened during dancing that as they say in the romance novels, he's not just looking at me, he's looking at ALL of me. I'm trying to deal with the sexual tension and still stay within the context of our relationship, meaning that when the band breaks, and Sly and I huddle together all sweaty on the dance floor (Arnold has deserted us to go home to Maria) I try to cool things down by talking about my Amazon detective story. "It's not just the premise that has to be great here, Sly," I tell him. "It's the solving of the case as well."

He gives me a look like he's going to smear me with cream and eat me up. But I'm the woman and it's my job to keep this stuff in check so I soldier on in the conversation. "The case came to me in a dream. It goes like this - Marga, our detective is hired by the Governor of Galatia to find his missing wife, Valentina Vesuvia."

Sly repeats the name Val-en-ti-na Ves-uv-i-a while tracing a pattern in an upward motion on the bare skin of my arm. Gee I find this distracting. "What was I talking about?" Sly moves closer to me and I can smell his Versace cologne. He takes my arm. "Let's get out of here."

I quite agree. On the way home, in the back of the limo, we make small talk but over the top of it I think about how I'm going to handle this. Under no circumstances I decide, will I make a first move. However if Sly's just absolutely insanely in love with me or something, then I am allowed a little fling, right? After all I am a woman, separated from a husband who has been cruel and inhumane.

When we get to the mansion, Slyvester leads me into the massive marble-floored living room with the giant palms. He walks behind the bar. "Want a drink?"

"Surprise me," I answer casually as I drift over to the big picture window and look out at the reflection of the moon in the pool while he shakes up something cool and frothy. I notice that Sly doesn't call in any of the servants, obviously wanting to protect our privacy. When he hands me my drink, he fixes me with his dark eyes and I'm locked in. I feel that same little shiver I always feel at the very top of the roller coaster ride.

"You know, Molly," he tells me "I'm the kind of man who likes to roam around." He moves closer to me. "I like changes, I like to meet new people."

"But you're loyal to Gianni Versace," I murmur.

"That's true."

"Seems to me that a man who can stick with the same designer shows great potential in the loyalty department."

The look on his face tells me that he has never really considered that. "What I'm trying to say Molly, is this ... I really like you and I want you to stay awhile. I'd like to have an office set up for you here so you can write your book and if you ever get stuck or need some advice, I'd like to help out. But you've got to understand that in creative and romantic matters, I'm kind of ...ephemeral."

"What do you mean?"

"Well, you know, my interests will change. I'll help you with the book, but then something else will happen and I'll have to move on."

He's so close to me. I try to remember if he's married right now. There was such a jumble of ex-wives and girlfriends and children at the party the other night.

"What could happen?"

Sylvester laughs, "Well, it's usually something beautiful, sometimes it's a piece of art, sometimes it's a movie deal, sometimes it's a woman." Sylvester puts down his drink. "It's just important that you know how I am."

He's so close and he smells so good. He puts his arms around me and he feels very big and warm and strong and I like this feeling alot. I lift my head so that our lips are just inches away. My eyes gaze into his and I forget to breathe....when the glass behind us shatters into a zillion pieces.

Chapter Seventeen

It seems like slow motion. First I hear the noise, then I turn my head to see the diamonds of broken glass come crashing onto Sly's marble floor, then behind the cascade of jagged glass, the dark figure of a man careens into the room. It's Dash. He's wearing a blue suit, white shirt, conservative tie and he's very angry. This makes me angry too.

Sly turns to face him standing perfectly balanced in a classic defensive position. "That was a mistake," he tells Dash as he backs a few steps to the bar, reaches around, and comes out with a whopping-size wooden ax handle.

I have to admit, I just love this. It's like having my own interactive movie screen. Unfortunately nobody else seems to be enjoying this as much as I am. Dash turns to me with a look that shows his clear expectation of an immediate explanation. Instead, I introduce him. "Sylvester, this is my husband Dashiel Denton."

"Molly, correct me if I'm wrong, but I don't remember your saying anything about a husband."

Well, he's got me there.

Dash turns to me and brushes the little pieces of glass from his suit. God, it's a beautiful suit -- dark blue, with that pale chalkline you can barely see, the kind you can only get in that really expensive fabric. I know I've never seen that suit in his closet. I know he had to get it just for this occasion, and I take a small perverse pleasure in that. Dash opens his hands and waves them in the air, expressing helpless male frustration. "How could you do this to me?" he asks in a voice choked with emotion.

This really irritates me. "What have I done to you, Dash?"

"Four children. Sixteen years of marriage and you've put me in a position where I have to break into another man's house to get you."

I am furious at the way Dash has cast everything in the light of how it relates to him. "This isn't about you, Dash. Actually this has almost nothing to do with you."

Meanwhile, Sylvester seems almost sympathetic to Dash, although I notice he still keeps his hand on the ax handle. I guess he's been in too many action movies to abandon the weapon. Sly frowns in thought. "How did you get by the dogs?" he asks Dash.

"I disconnected the electric fence, opened the gate, and threw fifteen pounds of tenderloin into the street."

"And the alarm system?"

"Disconnected," Dash tells Sly and then turns to me and makes a great show of rubbing his temples as if he's in pain. "Didn't you know that no matter where you went, I would find you?"

"Dash, I told you where I was. Remember the phone call?"

The most annoying thing about this entirely intrusive incident is that Sylvester is sympathetically listening to Dash during Dash's big phony wronged husband scene and at one point Sly actually begins to lower the ax handle to the floor. It bothers me intensely that Dash can command Sly's attention even the least little bit. "Dash, I'm here professionally. I'm working on a project with Sylvester. There's nothing else going on."

Sly nods. "That's true. I'm helping her with a story idea."

"Oh, give me a break," Dash says in a low, cracking voice.

Now I know that this is phony baloney, but Sylvester seems to think that Dash is actually upset over losing me. Dash should get an Oscar for this.

Sylvester rushes to explain to my husband how talented I am, not realizing, of course, that Dash has already reviewed my heroine, Margaret White, P.I. while searching the laundry room for clean socks. Dash listens to Sly, feigning interest, nodding here and there. But I've had enough of this. "I think it's time for you to go," I tell Dash who looks at me, takes a deep breath, and pretends to be suffering. I have to admit he looks pretty good in his banker's suit, but then I remind myself that Dash has always looked pretty good. It was never his appearance that was the problem, it was his behavior. "I'll leave if you want me to, Molly, but first I have something for you."

Dash walks across Sly's palatial living room, to the huge mahogany and teak wood front doors, opens one of them and goes outside for a few minutes. In bound Dash Jr, Bobby, Wayne, and Dart, laden with suitcases, hockey bags, and hockey sticks. They run up to me like a litter of puppies: hugging me, kissing me, practically jumping all over me. They shake hands with Sylvester, drop their suitcases and sports equipment, and begin looking around.

In the midst of all this, Dash walks out.

By the time I wake up, Sylvester is already swimming in the pool. From my window, I can see his tanned biceps glistening in the sun. I have to admit I'm a little worried about last night. Maybe now that I have become a family of five, I won't be quite as welcome in Casa Stallone.

I find a pair of scissors and do a serious cut-off job on my black jeans, tie my t-shirt into a knot under my midriff and study my reflection in the big floor-to-ceiling mirrors. I look small, almost fragile... a little woman with lots of rumpled hair. But I pull on my cowboy boots and go outside thinking, 'Well if he throws me out, he throws me out.'

I settle onto the English chintz cushions, study the graduations of color in the orchids and evaluate Sylvester's swimming technique. Eventually Sly gets out of the pool and pads over, dripping water onto the Italian mosaic tiled patio. He moves his chaise into the position of optimum sunlight and settles in. But before he closes his eyes to take some serious rays, he gives me one of those spiritually intimate glances that people around us last night were beginning to mistake for love. Then we accidentally and simultaneously quote Jimmy Buffet, "Just another shitty day in Paradise." I sigh because I know then that everything's going to be allright.

However I do have a little explaining to do so I tell Sly how I never actually abandoned my family, that I just took a little sabbatical in order to establish the creative atmosphere necessary to write my book. I feel it's important to explain this because Sly is Italian, and Italians are big on families. "I had some story ideas last night," I add.

"I like that, Molly." Sylvester turns his face toward the sun. "Work right through those personal problems. That's what I do too. Well...along with a little diversion."

Surreptitiously I check out his bronze muscles. Last night's little sizzle was obviously just temporary insanity. I'm sure he must have a wife or at least a girlfriend hovering nearby. As for me I'm only interested in my work.

"I decided that our detective Marga, hired by the Governor of Galatia, finds that the runaway wife - Valentina Vesuvia - has become a successful commodities trader in the grain market of Rome. This leaves Marga with an ethical dilemma of life or death proportions," I watch Sly's face carefully for signs of interest. "Should Marga tell her client, the Governor of Galatia the whereabouts of his wife, Valentina, which is her duty to her client but could result in a death sentence for Valentina due to the absolute power of the patriarchal monarch. Or does Marga follow a higher law and refuse to reveal anything?"

"Well that's a no-brainer. The Code of the Warrior, which is the basis for every action movie ever made, requires that Marga say no to the Governor."

"Right, so the Governor gets mad and order his men to kill Marga. Naturally Marga turns the table and executes the henchmen. Then she has to run for her life, which of course makes her a fugitive."

"Which is nice for a sequel," Sly points out.

"The only thing I haven't nailed is the sidekick. Every detective needs a sidekick."

"How about a retired Colosseum fighter?"

"Hmm, I like that." I can see from his eyes that he's intrigued.

"You know Molly," he hesitates. "I've got so much room on this property that your whole family can stay here. The boys can stay in the second guest house, and I'll set up an office for you in guest house three.... and then we can still work."

"Oh Sly, thank you. Nothing will change, I promise you."

At this point, a hockey puck whizzes by Sly's head less than an inch from his nose. Sly bravely refuses to flinch, or maybe the speed was such that there was no time to recoil. From the velocity of the puck, I recognize the most powerful shot in hockey: the slap shot with top velocities measuring around 110 miles per hour. I'm sure its proximity to Sylvester's head was just a mistake.

But next I hear the sound that has frightened me for years - a ferocious Siberian sound, the kind of sound you should never hear in a warm climate, not in Hawaii, not in Bermuda, and certainly not in Beverly Hills. It's the sound of street hockey. My four sons laughing, screaming, pushing, shoving, bumping, moaning, running, whooping make their way over to the tiled mosaic around the pool. They do not acknowledge us. They engulf us.

Although we are in danger, we stand our ground. We have to because if we move, they've won. And if they win today, tomorrow the mansion, the guest houses, the pool area, the entire compound will belong to them.

The puck, over which my sons are fighting, flies into the pool. My hope is that this will provide an interlude of quiet during which time Sylvester and I can make a safe exit. But my brood jump into the pool, fully clothed, hockey sticks flailing dangerously close to their skulls and dental work, while Dart screams like a Scottish banshee, "Pool hockey!!!!" After the period of time that it takes for them to realize that the water proposes an additional force of resistance against them, they crawl out of the pool and surround us, dripping all over Sly and me, our books, our papers, our orange juice in lovely Waterford goblets.

Dart starts in on me. "Hey, Mom, what's for breakfast? I'm starving."

Then Dash Jr, the family barrister, takes over. "What are we going to do around here? I mean we can't swim all day."

Wayne and Bobby are silent. They can afford to be with a brother who can turn a simple conversation into a moot trial competition. Besides they have each other to punch around over by the English orchids. I frown at the crew and try to sound authoritative. "Did you bring your school books?"

"Dad told us to, but we ditched them in Chicago," Dart volunteers proudly.

Jr. starts in on me again. "What's the competitive level of the hockey teams out here? Like what percentage are rated AAA? I'll bet there aren't any." Being the oldest and the closest to me emotionally, Dash, Jr. doesn't like me to miss any of his myriad thoughts and emotions, especially the negative ones. I remember this from my former life, which I have categorized as B.C. (Before California.) Mercifully Snake appears with a case of juice packs, which my sons inhale. I smile weakly at Sylvester, who pats my arm sympathetically.

When the drinking slows down, Sylvester addresses the crew using his low, throaty, threatening John Rambo voice. "Okay guys, here's the way it is. Snake is going to keep you busy today while your mother works. You will obey Snake completely. If you do everything you are supposed to do, I'll introduce you to Wayne Gretsky."

I think this may be the only time all four of my sons have been quiet at the same time. "You know Gretsky?" Dart finally squeaks.

"Absolutely," Sly tells him. "Snake, take them over to the south lawn for a while, so Molly and I can finish talking," Sly says, careful to maximize his advantage here.

The boys get up quietly and evaluate Snake, gauging his height, which is something around six feet, six inches, studying his shoulders, admiring his tattoos. All in all they seem quite pleased with their babysitter. When they are far enough away that he thinks he can risk it, Dart turns and yells happily. "Thanks, Mr. Stallone. This guys's gonna make a hell of a goalie."

With this kind of child care I think I may actually be able to work. However Lips finds me and reminds me that I have an appointment with Wicked Eric.

Thoughtfully, Sly has offered me his personal home gymnasium as a training site. As I walk down the long hallway, adorned with real Picassos, real Van Goghs and real Bruegels, I realize that I have been in most of the rest of Sly's house but never in the inner sanctum...the gym.

When I push open the carved mahogany door and enter, I'm glad to see that Eric hasn't arrived yet because it gives me a moment to get my bearings. The gym is very bright because all the walls are mirrored. Many different kinds of weight training equipment along with weight belts and little baskets of chalk sit on the rich red oriental carpets. There are a few sculptures of beautiful bodies, mostly torsos.

At any rate it's an humbling place. And I barely have time to get my intimidation factor in check before Wicked Eric comes in the door wearing cut-off zebra tent pants and one of those gym tees with the great big armholes. Despite the ridiculous lifter outfit he looks just as incredibly handsome as he did the last time we met. He carries in boxes of vitamin supplements and big cylinders of that soy branching amino acid stuff. He's also brought a large poster which he proceeds to unroll. "Now you know I'm not crazy about building the female body..."

I nod because I do feel that he made this perfectly clear in our previous meeting.

"...but I've been rethinking my position and doing a little research and I've decided that Rachel...." At this point he fully unrolls a life size posing photograph of former Ms. Olympia, Rachel McLish. He pulls a roll of tape from his pocket and proceeds to tape this poster up on one of the mirrors. I'm wondering if Sly is going to allow this intrusion on his personal domain but Eric is unconcerned. He steps back and admires the giant muscled female form.

"Rachel McLish," Eric tells me solemnly, "is almost perfect."

Although I've never really liked the look of female body builders, I do have to admit that Rachel looks pretty swell wearing her tiny silver posing bikini.

Of course I know I'll never look like that because I know that my forty year old body will resist all of Eric's best efforts to remold it into another form. One of the reasons I went along with this weight training is that I know nothing will happen to my body except for the existing muscle to tone - slightly.

Of course Eric, the expert in the aesthetics of muscular proportions, doesn't realize this yet. I know because he tells me, "Rachel is almost perfect. I can make you absolutely perfect."

I would laugh but the intensity in his eyes and the urgency in his voice stop me.

Chapter Eighteen

It doesn't take long for me to acclimate to my luxurious surroundings at Casa Stallone and the days begin to slide into one another. Before the L.A. sky is bright over the chlorinated waters and the rattling palms, Arnold has telephoned me. "Wake up! Don't sleep your life away!" he enthuses Germanically over the phone. He's developing an annoying habit of doing this at precisely 5:30 every morning. However I have accepted his eccentricity, and usually follow his wake up call with a period of writing in my great new office in Guest House 3 where I have my monster IBM computer, fax/ modem, CD-Rom research library, coffee pot, refrigerator, paper shredder, and wall safe (Sly has instructed me to lock up my pages and floppy disks every night because you can't be too careful around here.)

Later poolside, Sly (concentrating on the mentor thing) teaches me the Code of the Warrior. He instructs me that every action movie or heroic saga must dramatize the code, meaning that it must open with the action-warrior completely alone and close with the action-warrior exultant and victorious but still emotionally separated from the weave of society. And that no matter what sub-plots I blend into my story, the action line of my hero Marga must always dominate all other story elements.

This morning I watch Sly as he reads my latest descriptive passage. It's true that I am a bit smug about this elegant three-page segment on the nutrition of the average Roman citizen. But Sly isn't thrilled. When he's done reading he looks over at me, fixes me with the big browns, and asks, "Geez, Molly, when is something going to happen here?"

Naturally I kill the passage immediately.

When Sylvester stands up, the brilliant morning light backlights the contours of his muscular body creating the multicolored prismatic effect of an aura. I suppose I could be imagining this but it seems perfectly real to me.

After our morning talk, I weight train with Eric and then squeeze in an aerobics session on the south lawn because Mary Pat Johannsen is there and I want another opportunity to touch her in order to keep the telepathic magic alive. So I aerobicize right next to Mary Pat and faking an ankle sprain, fall into her.

Following the exercise, I retrieve my sons from Sylvester's kitchen, which is where they eat breakfast. Me, I don't eat breakfast anymore, not since Eric restructured my nutritional needs. Now I take a lot of pills, drink green pine milkshakes and chew on crunchy things that taste like petrified popcorn. Of course, I am thinking of chocolate all the time. I herd the boys over to Victor Vann, who I greet every day with a rag and a rub. It's a morning ritual for me to shine up some little part of Victor. Big, safe, and reliable, Victor went across the whole country for me, and I do not forget my friends. Of course I had to give Sly a little cover story about Victor. I told him that I bought Victor at a BATF sale of used vehicles. Initially I was worried about the bodyguards ratting me out but when I discovered their memories were as short as their attention spans, I knew everything would be okay.

When the boys are done with breakfast, I fire up Victor and drive the kids to Pacific Heights Academy, an excellent private school Sylvester found for us. The academy is small and exclusive, admits grades one through twelve, and boasts several hockey teams. On the way, my sons relate to me their pressing concerns. "We need air casts for wrists and twenty-three plastic hamster houses, tubes and plastic caps." Dart tells me. "The hamsters have run out of living space and we're going to expand their habitat."

"But there's only five of them."

"Not anymore," Dart says proudly.

I think about requesting the current total of hamster population but change my mind. In this new town, without friends, the boys haven't had much to do and have filled their time with endless trips to the pet shop on Wilshire for more hamsters. Who would have known that there are so many varieties - from teddy bear to hairless, from Chinchilla to Chinese? But this collection of rodents keeps them busy so I laugh a Donna Reed laugh and promise to take them for hamster building supplies after school.

Finally free of my progeny, I settle down again in my office with all my high tech accoutrements (In addition to the goodies Sly provided for me, I also arranged for an internet connection and a special T-1 phone line so that I could research large amounts of historical material.) After a very long day's work, I accumulate a respectable twenty pages, and while sitting dazed and satisfied in front of my computer, I get a vision. It must be a Mary Pat Johannsen Vision (MPJV) because as I sit at my computer screen in my office in L.A., what I see is my home in Maine. Specifically I see my laundry room, which is where I have always kept my computer. And the view I have is what I would see if I were in the exact position of the computer, which leads me to believe that I am seeing through the screen of the computer, the big blue eye of the computer.

I wonder how I can look into a computer screen in Beverly Hills and see into my home in Bangor, Maine. This defies logic and the laws of nature. On the other hand, it does offer me new information. I notice that the laundry room door is open and I can see right into the recreation room.

Dash and his best friend and neighbor Mitchell Richmond are sitting at the poker table. In front of them are several empty Coors bottles. Fortunately the volume is low enough that I can hear Mitch tell Dash, "I can't believe you did it."

Dash sticks out his chin. "It had to be done."

"But why didn't you talk to me first? You're always supposed to talk to me before you make a move." Mitch has been Dash's lawyer for the construction company for years and Dash has gotten into the habit of reviewing all his decisions with him.

"What for?"

"Well, I hate to break this to you, but that was not the smartest move in the world - legally."

Dash shrugs. "So what?"

"Don't you realize you just gave her custody?"

"It was a spur of the moment thing."

"You didn't plan to do it?"

"Well...not exactly."

"Then why did you go? Were you trying to get her back?"

I can see from the hurt look in Dash's eyes that Mitch has hit upon the truth. But Dash looks away and curls his lower lip into a sneer. "Everything I do, Mitch, is calculated to give me the upper hand. The name of the game here isn't custody."

"Oh yeah, what's the name of the game?"

"It's called 'Who's on Top.'"

Mitch takes off his glasses and cleans them with the tail of his shirt. "Look, why don't you just let me take this over for you?"

"I know exactly what I'm doing," Dash insists. "How long do you think Molly's going to last in L.A. with the four boys? There's no decent hockey in Southern California."

"So you think she'll be coming home soon?"

"Of course."

"Well it's not how I would handle it, but I have to admire your composure. You're dead calm, all right."

"This is a crisis. I have to be calm."

"Sure."

"She'll be back... I was down in the first period, but I'm coming back in the second. I have everything going for me."

"Okay."

"Mitch, I feel like all the forces of human nature are working in my favor." Dash clenches his fist for emphasis. The screen fades to that pretty Caribbean blue and I realize that I was right about him all along.

To Dash, everything is a game.

I ruminate on this for a while before it's time for Sly and I to enjoy another of our rituals. Because bodies of water attract high levels of negative ions which are great for the creative juices of the right brain, we like to have dinner by the pool. Ordinarily our dinner would be followed by another lifting session with Eric who claims you can lift twice a day as long as you're working different muscles, but I cancelled our session tonight because Sly has invited me and the boys to meet some producer friends of his. Unfortunately my cancellation so irritated Eric that he threatened me with failure to reach perfection unless I meet his every nutrition and lifting demand in the future.

The boys are so happy to have something to do, that they mill around the limo like excited puppies. When we all pile into the stretch limo, Snake drives us down Sly's driveway past his security cameras and through his electronic gate. Then he drives the three hundred feet to the next electronic gate with security cameras mounted on both sides. After announcing ourselves and gaining entry we drive up our neighbor's driveway, next to which the dog trainers are calling in the Doberman's.

A tall English butler leads us inside the Mock-English Tudor mansion and announces us to Sam Selig and his wife, Candy. Sam is a little man with lots of body hair poking out of his shirt's collar and sleeves. He's about sixty while his wife Candy, a vivacious honey blonde looks more like thirty.

Candy shows us into a large screening room where we all sit down on the overstuffed contemporary sofas that face a giant movie screen. I figure we're going to see a film but the screen begins to lift and this exposes a wall of glass which I look through - and gasp.

I can't believe what I'm seeing. On the other side of the glass, in its own pristine, protected, air-conditioned glory, is my old nemesis: The ice. Around the rink, a big black and white Zamboni cleans the surface. Waiting for the Zamboni to finish are several boys in full equipment. I turn to Candy, "Your sons?'

"Sam's sons from wife number 2," she sets me straight. "I'm wife number 3. My babies are upstairs with their nannies." My sons immediately begin a low growl of excitement and discharge many undecipherable phrases in that new high-tech trash talk they all use, when a tall figure glides onto the ice... a tall familiar figure. My four sons are completely silent.

Finally Dart recovers his voice. "It's Wayne - Wayne Gretsky."

Sly smiles. "That's the way it's done, Molly. Set it up - pay it off. That's what we've been talking about every morning." It strikes me then that my friend Sylvester could be the absolute antithesis of minimalism and that could be the reason I'm here.

Sly directs Snake to bring over the boy's hockey equipment and then engages in a little man-to-man with Sam about real estate values, art, and the relative merits of rottweilers versus dobermans.

Meanwhile Candy and I fall into a neighborly talk. She invites me over for coffee sometime, so I invite her to come over for a swim sometime. Then she offers to give me the name of her masseuse, manicurist, and aromatherapist. She also invites me to join her for her daily Ta'i chi instruction with Master Wong, who teaches the Chi on the ice, and entirely in Cantonese. Candy explains that the Chi is actually a more interesting discipline on the ice since the matter of balance is entirely different. What really appeals to me however is learning Cantonese since I can't help feeling that my foreign language skills have been deteriorating since I left my Russian instructor behind in Maine. As for going out on the ice, well let's just I'm say I'm not crazy about it.

"Come tomorrow night," Candy suggests but I have to say maybe and explain my writing schedule to her. She scrunches up her pretty face in thought, "Well you're going to need a good agent."

"Sly thinks Elliot Stanton."

"Okay, but you're also going to need a good publicist. And don't use Sly's guy Bernie because he's too conservative. Bernie's good at converting negative publicity to positive publicity, which is great if you're already a mogul. But when you're just breaking in, you need a hungry, amoral, almost desperate publicist and that means..." She chews on a strand of her honey colored hair. "McTeague... Yes, McTeague's a hyperthyroid and they always make the best publicists. The only hitch with McTeague is that he operates out of Ivans which is actually a hairdressing salon." When she sees the surprised look on my face she smiles mischievously, "But don't worry it's the absolute center of the social and professional universe."

I decide that I like this woman. She's seems to be a wise old crone wrapped up in a buff Southern California body. And since she seems to know everything about everybody I ask her for advice about my problem with Wendy Kroy.

"Oh, my God!" her eyed widen. "You shouldn't have talked about your story in public. Don't you know what it's like around here? It's so bad that everybody has their homes and offices and cars swept for bugs once a week."

"Isn't that kind of paranoid?"

"You'd better forget about that Amazon story and write something else instead."

I consider her advice but my natural literary confidence takes over. "Wendy Kroy can't write my story." I say petulantly.

"No," Candy agrees. "But she can steal it."

Chapter Nineteen

I'm eating Eric's seaweed green popcorn and working on my first narrative book, which is where the young Marga is captured by a band of slavers. My usual way of working is to first decide on the tone and general direction, then I do the dialogue, and after that I fill in the descriptions.

But for some reason this time, I find myself seeing the story in very precise visuals. I see it as a series of vignettes in golden tones rather like the old Victor Mature Colosseum epics. I see lots of dust, feet in leather sandals, plenty of bronzed oiled muscles misted to show sweat. But instead of the brilliant blue sky of the old movies, I see a dark steely sky combined with an ominous sound track of discordant computer music suggesting the harshness of life.

Thoughts like these make it hard for me to work and I'm struggling to formulate my concept and direction with all these pictures filling my head when the scene changes and I find myself looking into a joint with a bamboo bar and fake palm trees. Dash and Mitch are drinking. I wonder what they're doing at this place with palm trees when I hear the sugary background music of the Bee Gees and I realize they're at the Big Pineapple, a tacky pick -up spot on Route 88.

This time I'm not touching the telephone or seeing through the computer screen. This time the vision is all around me, a kind of MPJ virtual reality and I feel like I'm really there as Dash leans over the bar. "Come on, let's blow this joint," he slurs his words just enough so that I can tell he's plastered.

"But the set's not over." Mitch looks nervous. Maybe he's afraid Barb will find out. She doesn't like him out anywhere with Dash because she feels Dash is a bad influence and she's right.

"So we'll play the C.D. at home," Dash stands up and reaches out.

Then I see why Mitch is nervous. Because the thing that Dash has reached out to get is a little blonde. She grabs her purse and stands next to Dash like he's a big C.E.O. or something. You know the body language, "I'm just so cute and thrilled to be here with the big man." I thought it went out in high school, but apparently it's still alive in retro low-life establishments like the Big Pineapple.

To my credit, I am not surprised at this. Nor am I angry or jealous. I hate Dash, of course, but that's nothing new. I've known for a long time what a scum sucking, borderline mentally impaired, poor excuse for a male genital organ, he is. But I am not surprised, angry or jealous.

Dash pulls the bimbo toward the door. "You want to go ice skating?" he asks.

"Ice skating...at this time of night?" She sounds like Betty Boop. But I guess when you're blonde and wearing a low-cut fake leopard-skin dress, it doesn't really matter what you sound like.

"In my backyard," Dash insists.

Her over-mascaraed little eyes light up. I guess she figures she's got a big one on the line. She doesn't know he's a garbage sucking bottom fish. "That's a good one." She laughs a little tinkly laugh. "I've heard a lot of lines but ice skating in the backyard? That's good. Sure, let's go."

Dash calls over to Mitch, who is still sitting at the bar. "Come on, Mitch, we're leaving."

"This is really a great little band," Mitch stalls. "Let's stay for the next set." Good old Mitch, always trying to avoid trouble.

But Dash ignores him and heads outside with the blonde. Reluctantly Mitch pays the check and follows them out. It's a beautiful summer night, bright with a full moon and the smell of honeysuckle and I am momentarily homesick for Maine.

"Oooh, I love vans," Betty Boop croons. "What'cha got inside?"

Dash leans close to her. "Everything."

Reluctantly Mitch gets out the keys and opens up the van. As the blonde gets in, Mitch takes Dash's arm, pulls him away from the van, and tells him, "I'm not driving her to your house."

"Afraid of my wife? Or afraid of your wife?"

Mitch frowns and I can appreciate his dilemma. If I were him, I wouldn't want to risk this getting back to Barb either. "Let's just drive the lady home," he suggests.

Mitch starts up the big conversion van and drives for a while. In the middle of asking Betty Boop her address for at least the third time, Dash interrupts him by commanding, "Home, Mitchell," and for a brief moment, I wonder if this little scenario is going to end up with Betty Boop in my bed. And if it does, what will I do?

Shall I be pro-active? Shall I fly back across the country, taxi to the house, take the 30:06 down from the gun rack, load her up and murder Dash? After all, it's half my house. He's still my husband. If I was a man in Italy I could get away with it.

But Dash sees something out the window. "Uh-oh, wait a minute... turn left." Dash continues to stare intently at something. "Stop at the third house on the right." Mitch stops and Dash stumbles a little as he gets out of the van and walks up to the front door of a large brick house.

I know this house because this is the house that I visited weekly for almost a year. This is the home of Dr. Gita Haboudange, the home of in-his-face therapy.

Dash rings the bell. It's the middle of the night and the house is dark, and Gita's voice comes over the intercom. "Who is it?" she asks in her sleepy yet powerful Middle Eastern voice.

"It's Dash Denton."

"Who?"

"Dash Denton, Molly's Denton's husband."

"What do you want?" Gita sounds suspicious.

"I just want to talk to you about my wife."

"What happened to Molly?"

"She ran away to L.A. and she's living with Sylvester Stallone."

The front door opens. Gita in her robe and slippers is peering out behind the safety chain. "I know she had that recurring dream, but I never thought..."

"What recurring dream?"

"The Sulvester Stallone dream. To tell you the truth, I completely disregarded it. It never occurred to me that it was some form of obsession."

"This is no dream. This is real. Molly is out there in L.A. writing a book with this guy or so she says."

Gits shakes her head. "I'm speechless."

"You should be. You've ruined my life." Dash's face is twisted in a mean, half drunken frown. "I'm going to sue you. There's got to be some form of legal compensation available. My lawyer is in the van over there."

Gita ignores that. "Is there a number where I can reach Molly?"

"You see the blond woman in the van?" Dash waves his arm toward Mitch's van.

"I'm going to take her home right now and I'm going to take her up to my wife's bedroom. I'm going to give her one of my wife's negligees and then ... then I'm going to commit adultery."

I make up my mind right then and there that if he gives Betty Boop my Gillian O'Malley nightgown, I will definitely murder him with the 30.06. But Dash is continuing on in his more or less drunken slur. "And when Molly comes home, begging me to take her back..."

"You think that will happen?" Gita asks.

"Absolutely and when it does..."

But Gita interrupts him again. "What's Molly's number?'

"That does it." Dash walks away shaking his head and as he walks toward the van, a taxi pulls up. Mitch puts the blonde in the cab and it takes off. Dash rushes over to Mitch. "Are you nuts?"

"I used the car phone to call her a cab."

Dash's arrogant sneer softens and dissolves. "Geez, she was so pretty. Didn't she look like Molly? I mean her eyes. Didn't her eyes remind you of Molly?"

My original plan was to finish my book and then worry about marketing. But based on the fact that the assemblage of a brilliant marketing team takes time, Sly and Arnold have strongly suggested that the best time to start is somewhere between the beginning and the middle.

Because he is based in L.A. and represents West Coast commercial writers while still maintaining clients and connections among the New York Literati, we've all agreed that the best literary agent for my work is the brother of Erwin Stanton - Elliot Stanton. That's why my short stories as well as an extensive outline of <u>Marga, Amazon Detective</u> were messengered over to him a week ago and I have an appointment with him this morning.

High above the Mercedes and Jaguars and Mia Miatas, even higher than the Range Rovers, I maneuver Victor Van down Wilshire in the direction of Stanton's office. Sly calls me on the car phone and detects a nervous quaver in my voice. "I think I have performance anxiety," I tell him.

"What's performance anxiety?"

I figure he must be joking, right? But I explain to him that I'm kind of nervous that maybe Elliot Stanton won't like me or my work and that I'm afraid I won't be able to convince him to take me as a client.

Sylvester switches to that slur he uses for the movies. "Well Moll, you don't have to knock the guy out, you just have to go the distance." Then he lets his voice return to normal. "Seriously would you like Arnold and me to stop by after our workout? We could do that." That was sweet but I politely decline.

As I drive up to the impressive Frank Gehry building that houses Stanton's literary agency, I remember the words of Andre Agassi, "Image is Everything." After parking the van, I take a deep breath and try to put confidence in my walk. The trendy glass block elevator takes me up to the sixth floor and after a short wait, I am shown into the office.

Elliot Stanton gets up from his Palazetti glass-top desk to greet me. He's twig-thin and wears a charcoal tweed jacket by A. Soprani with a coordinating charcoal turtleneck. Horn-rim Oliver Peoples glasses sit on his long straight nose. Behind him the shades of gray used on the walls and furnishings blend into a montage of tone on tone.

On the walls of Elliot's office is the work of David Onica, Lichtenstein, and David Hockney, as well as a few trophy photos of Elliot with Jay MacInerney, Elliot with Bret Easton Ellis, Elliot with one of the Hemingway granddaughters, and a charcoal caricature of the Stanton brothers one on each coast, inscribed "Together we control Kansas."

After extending his bony hand to me, Elliot gestures toward the chocolate brown leather Eames across from his desk. When he speaks his voice is soft, his words precise, and it's pretty clear he's not crazy about my short stories because he calls them 'very Northeastern' in a tone of voice that's ever so slightly a dump, a diss, a put-down.

Not that I care what he thinks of my short stories because I don't like them either. It's Margaret White transmogrified into Marga the Amazon detective that I care about. But Elliot wants to explain to me how my minimalist short stories can be improved and he wants to do this at great length. I try to distract him by throwing out a Hemingway quotation, "Good writers only compete with the dead."

But Elliot doesn't want to play Hemingway and the ringing telephone interrupts us. When Elliot answers, we are both surprised that the phone call is for me. I put the receiver to my ear and listen to an agitated yet vaguely familiar voice, "Molly, I'm at Yale. Why aren't you here?"

For a moment, I'm confused but then I remember the April 25th promise to read at Yale with Gordon Durkee. "Gordon, is that you? How did you find me?" I ask, annoyed at whoever gave him this number. He starts to reply but I realize I have to hang up on him.

Right now it's more important that I take control of Elliot and lay down my terms and I just don't have time to rehash yesterday's news with Gordon. "The short stories are no longer for sale," I tell Elliot, "because I'm in the middle of a new work now. It's about a hero's struggle and the transformation of character in the crucible of action. I believe that's the outline on your desk." I ought to recognize the outline, considering all the extra time I've spent on it.

"Yes..." Elliot licks his lips and adjusts his glasses. "Yes, I remember, it's an action/detective story ...with a heroine?" he says with just the slightest edge of incredulity.

"Is that a problem for you, Elliot?"

"Of course not," Elliot stammers in his rush to get the words out. "I have never favored any particular race or creed or gender."

"I'm working in the grand romantic style of Gaddis, Heller, Pynchon, and Mailer." I have to cross my fingers here in hopes that I can even come anywhere near the work of Gaddis, Heller, Pynchon, and Mailer. "I have five major plots, seventeen subplots, multiple thematic development..."

"Yes... it's an action/epic/romantic/saga/detective story?"

"Exactly."

Elliot turns the top few pages of my very extensive outline and then flips through several pages of computer print out that sits on his desk.

"You know, your project sounds an awful lot like one just accepted by my colleague, Paul Murfman."

"What?"

Elliot searches for the right page. "Here it is - the heroine, a private detective in ancient Rome, is descended from a small band of Amazons who have been living in isolation for centuries."

"That's my story." I protest, I mean how many other people could have thought that up."

Elliot takes off his Oliver People's glasses and massages the bridge of his long English nose. "Well, I'm afraid I'll have to pass on your project due to our previous commitment."

Because my mouth is still gaping open in disbelief, Elliot tries to soften the blow, "Very often two artists are working on similar projects at the same time. A long time ago, I decided that such things are simply cosmic coincidence."

I manage a dry whisper. "Who's the author?"

"Actually this was presented by an independent producer, who hasn't credited the writer.

"So who's the producer?"

Chapter Twenty

Wendy Kroy!

I'm speechless. How could she have worked up my idea and gotten it to a literary agent before me? And how will I ever convince Elliot Stanton that Marga, the Amazon detective is my story, and that I am the only one who can write it?

At this moment, there is a knock at the half-open door and contrary to my instructions, we are joined by Sly and Arnold. They are both freshly endorphined and showered and no doubt throwing off halos of good pheromones from their workout. Sly in his black silk Versace looking very European and Arnold in his American look, wheat-colored L.L. Bean. Together they seem like two massive bookends. And even though I told them not to come, I am so glad to see them.

Sly must have heard some of my conversation with Elliot because as he lowers his muscular frame into a chair, he says the five magic words to Elliot. "We're going to film it."

Elliot looks back and forth from Sylvester to Arnold. I study Elliot's expression for signs of the synapsing of his brain as he figures out how he's going to screw Paul Murfman. But his face is as smooth as a pool's surface and all he says is "Oh, the film connection is definite?"

"Absolutely," Sly replies.

I guess a book project with a film deal is just too commercially attractive to turn down, at least initially because Elliot stands up, smiles broadly, and shakes hands all around. "I'd like to see progressive sections of the manuscript as you move along," he tells me.

"Thank God," I mutter as the three of us squeeze into the little glass elevator. My teeth are chattering by the time we get to the street probably due to the adrenaline rush that accompanied my fear that Wendy had beaten me out.

She's fast, I think, incredibly fast. She must have lots of people working for her - people who don't sleep or eat. In a rush I try to explain to Sly and Arnold how this Wendy Kroy connection came about, how Wendy cornered me at Sly's party and how Wendy was eavesdropping on me at the coffee shop on Rodeo Drive.

"Relax and slow down," Arnold complains because I'm talking too fast. "This kind of thing happens all the time out here. Everything will be allright. Just remember that whenever you're faced with a challenge, you must mentally go right back to the Code of the Warrior. Now how many pages have you written?" Arnold asks.

"I don't know."

"You're a writer and you don't know how many pages you've written?"

I don't want to answer this directly, so I fudge, "I'm well along. I'll be done in no time."

"Molly, you have to keep your mind on production and maintain your focus."

Sly agrees, "You should listen to Arnold. He's talking about the Code of the Warrior. He's talking about going the distance." They both look me over carefully like they're evaluating my receptivity to this advice. Apparently I fail because Sylvester says, "We'd better continue this discussion back at the ranch," and Arnold agrees with him.

Sly insists that I ride back with them in the limo and I don't object even though it means that one of the bodyguards will have to drive Victor Van home later, because after all, Sly and Arnold just came to my rescue with Elliot Stanton. As we drive along I think about what Arnold said about my page production and I have to admit that while I started writing Marga with an average daily page production of about twenty, it quickly dropped to about ten, and even then most of the work went into the outline which was over a hundred pages long. So I can't even say I ever really established a great forward momentum.

As we drive by a row of giant starburst palms, I notice a long black limo streaking past us and although I only get a sideways glimpse of the driver I am certain from the profile that it's Wicked Eric. This makes me uncomfortable, even though I know that driving is Eric's second job. I can't help wondering if he's checking up on me. Would he actually take the time to follow me around? Naah, that's crazy, I decide.

When we get back to the compound, Sly leads us to the weight room, which is, in my opinion, a poor choice for a conference because there are no chairs. Sly and Arnold both stand in exactly the same position, feet slightly apart, stomachs sucked in, shoulders squared - kind of like the 'at ease' position in the military. Naturally I assume the same position.

"You did not demonstrate confidence in Elliot's office," Arnold tells me and I'm sure he's right about that. "It's okay to feel nervous. But it's not okay to act nervous. Remember you must never show weakness. <u>Never</u>. No matter how bad the situation, no matter how humiliating or how imminent the loss appears to be, your face must be cool as a block of ice, your body as still as frozen pond. Let me demonstrate..." Arnold composes himself into a solid muscular statute, and then ever so slightly turns his massive jawline like he's going to deliver a line of dialogue. He turns to Sylvester, "Now you show her."

Sylvester demonstrates stillness by twisting himself into a Rodin-like pose, throwing just a hint of disdain into his glance and an almost imperceptible curl into his upper lip. Even though neither one of them has a weapon, they both manage to look very dangerous.

But now it's Sylvester's turn. "What else have you learned about the Warrior Code?"

I sigh, thinking that if I'm going to be tested, I would prefer multiple choice questions. I shift my weight from one foot to the other.

But Sylvester answers for me, "You must maintain your focus and drive. If you maintain your own focus and drive, you never even have to think about the competition because you have already left them in the dust." He looks at me expectantly.

"Okay."

"The warrior knows that in order to win, he has to play his own game."

Gee, that sounds familiar. I think I heard that on one of Dash's hockey coaching cassettes. It didn't seem to have anything to do with writing a book then and it doesn't now. They're starting to lose me with this macho stuff and I'm getting kind of hungry for dinner and it's occurring to me that these two could go on like this for a very long time when fortunately Sylvester brings the conversation around to the subject of endings. Now that's a more interesting subject than 'play your own game.' So I encourage him by throwing out a quotation, "Great is the art of beginning, but greater is the art of ending, Thomas Fuller."

"Ending," Sly responds, "It's pure instinct, Harold Pinter." We toss quotations back and forth. Both of us are so well read, that by the time we exhaust our mutual supply of quotes, Arnold has gotten bored and excused himself to get home to Maria.

So Sly and I take our friendly game of dueling quotations to some comfortable chairs by the pool, eventually working our way through dinner and onto the specifics of my Marga story. The one thing we agree upon is that if the beginning is the most important part of a story, then surely the ending is the second most important part. Sylvester points out that since my Marga story is a warrior saga, it must have a warrior ending, which can vary from glorious total victory to a bare bones survival ending.

But I think his point of view is a little simplistic. I feel that anyone who has gone on a vicarious journey with me, is entitled to be uplifted in some manner at the end. I don't care what kind of story it is. This is my basic bottom line regarding my work. But it's been a long day and I'm all talked out. Furthermore Sly seems worried that I'm going to screw up the ending by getting preachy or corny or romantic or moralistic.

"Preachy, corny, romantic, or moralistic? Moi?" I tell him, but he doesn't look convinced.

"Remember, Molly, romance and ethical conflict are great as subplots. But if you spend too much story time on them or plaster on an uplifting ending, our epic action saga will turn into a character drama." His look clearly tells me that this is a nauseating proposition.

"Quit worrying Sylvester," I reassure him. "Just because I added a little subplot where Marga has the hots for her sidekick Aurelius is no reason to lose confidence in me. You haven't lost confidence in me, have you?"

"Naah," he reaches over and takes a big drink of mineral water. "I guess I'm just surprised at how fast you're putting this thing together. At the rate you're going, you'll be done in no time."

Now I could correct him at this point because it's clear that Sly thinks we've been discussing endings because I'm near the end of my story. And the fact is that I haven't even broken one hundred pages. I think about telling him this and detailing my reasons which are all really good. For instance there's the fact that I had to spend so much time on the one hundred and thirty page outline for Elliot Stanton. And there's the fact that I've decided to polish my prose as I go along which has led me to start every work day rewriting yesterday's pages. But as I'm sitting there, I realize that anything I say will sound like an excuse and I really don't feel like making excuses. In fact, if I'm understanding today's lesson correctly I'm never, ever supposed to show weakness.

So why on earth should I admit that after all this time, I'm only on page 89. In fact such an admission seems to me to be a definite sign of weakness. So I compose myself into a cool ethereal pose and knowing that my compliance with Sly's misunderstanding is really a deception, I just let him think whatever he wants.

"C'mon, let's take a walk," I suggest, suddenly taken with an urge to move around.

"On the street?"

"No, no, around the property." As we head out past the Italian vineyard, the olive trees from Crete, and twist around past the English orchids I notice through the foliage and electrified iron fencing, that a long black limo is sitting, with the motor running, across the street from Sylvester's mansion. When I point this out to Sly he says, "Geez Molly, it's only a limo. Limos are all over."

At my urging, we walk a little closer and I peer into the driver's window, all the while thinking, No, it can't be. But it is. "It's Eric," I gasp. "What's he doing out there?"

"Picking somebody up?" Sylvester still seems unconcerned.

"But he's parked across the street from your house in the middle of the night. Don't you find that crazy?"

"Naah, strange people are always parked in front of my house. That's my life."

I look at the long dark car idling across the street. Even though at one time, I was one of those people parked in front of Sly's house, I don't feel good about this.

Chapter Twenty-One

"Molly, everything in this world is either sex or money, and you don't have any money. So who've you screwed since you got here?"

I shake my head.

"Maybe you accidentally screwed somebody really powerful, somebody so powerful that he told Sylvester and Arnold to help you. Think back."

"I would have remembered that."

Barb narrows her eyes. "So why are they helping you?"

"Because they're nice guys?"

"Molly, come on."

"Because I have a great personality?"

Barb laughs incredulously.

"Because they like my work?"

Barb waves her well manicured hands in the air. "Look I don't want to argue. Just drag Sly out here and introduce me."

But Barb has to wait. She spends the night in my guest house sleeping the deep sleep of jet lag. I know because I'm up creeping around with insomnia all night which has been happening more and more often lately. The next day Barb is fresh and perky, while I have to down three cappuccinos just to get going.

"I have an appointment this morning, want to come?" I offer.

"What I want, is to meet Sylvester," One thing abut Barb, she's persistent.

"First things first. I'm interviewing a public relations agent who I might hire to do some work for me."

She hesitates, "It's a business interview?"

"Yeah, but it's at a beauty parlor. Cmon, you'll love it."

And she does. The samovars glisten and the Russian wolfhounds run freely through the salon at Ivan's, hairstylist to the stars. As the dour receptionist wearing a severe pre-glasnost gray suit summons us from the waiting room, I have a moment when I question my own judgment. Sure, I want the hungriest, the sharkiest publicist on the face of the earth, but I do find it strange to be conferencing in a beauty parlor. Even though Ivan's is an expensive beauty parlor with an upscale Euro-trash decor, still I hate beauty parlors second only to ice rinks.

Apparently there has been some mistake made here because the receptionist insists that I am scheduled for Ivan to "do" me this morning; nose to toes, that is "full body treatment." I get out several sentences in Russian each one beginning with "Nyet," but the receptionist tells me that anyone who wants to see McTeague has to see Ivan first. And anyone who comes to Ivan's for the first time has to have the "full body treatment."

Obviously these terms are ridiculous and I explain this to the receptionist. However she tells me that the terms are non-negotiable and I give in. My rationalization is that this is an opportunity to use the Russian I learned in Maine, and since Barb is practically hysterical with excitement at getting done at a really big, really L.A. salon, I figure I'll go with the flow here and they can "do" the both of us.

When they introduce me to Ivan I give him a well-pronounced "Zdrastveetyia" followed by "Menya zaboot Molly. Kak dela?"

Naturally he is charmed. Nothing warms the heart of a recent emigre more than hearing his own language. Ivan, who is just a short, nondescript man in a Russian military uniform, puffs out his chest and informs me that his full name is Ivan Ivanovitch. When I express surprise that he has the same name as the hero in a short story by Gogol, he tells me that it is no BFD (big fucking deal) because in Russia Ivan is as common as John. And since Ivanovitch means son of Ivan, Ivan Ivanovitch is just the Russian equivalent of John, Jr., which is something I hadn't ever considered. "Really," he tells me. "There would be lots of Ivan Ivanovitchs in the Russian phone books, if Russians had lots of phones."

Since Ivan has given me a new thought, I soften a little toward this guy who is after all just a haircutter out to make some big bucks. Besides, after my swim this morning, I soaked my hair in olive oil, just in case some overzealous hair tech were to try to sneak some peroxide-based color onto my hair. As I said, I don't trust beauty parlors.

At Ivan's the full body treatment is patterned after the European spas whose purpose is not to puritanically sweat and starve the body, but to pamper and indulge the body. So they start by packing Barb and me side by side in a big tub filled with blue black mud, calling it an Odessa mud bath. Supposedly it is filled with mud from the Black Sea. Yeah, right. Nevertheless as a writer, I like to feel I'm just as open to new experiences as say Hunter Thompson or William Burroughs, provided death, mutilation, and permanent injury are not involved.

Barb leans back as luxuriously as if they have placed her in Cleopatra's warm milk bath. Me, I sit there contemplating the odds that this is really mud from the Black Sea. Since the Russian have been free-dumping nuclear waste in the Black Sea for some time, I am hoping that this is not actually Russian mud but California mud. However I'm not too nervous about it because by estimating the cost of shipping the mud from Russian I calculate the odds against this stuff being genuine at about 500 to 1.

"This is great," Barb enthuses. "It's so L.A. I can't wait to tell them about this back home. Oh, is that Goldie Hawn?"

A mud-covered blonde raises herself from another smoking tub. She's completely unrecognizable, so I tell Barb, "No, that's Barbra Streisand." My Barb suppresses a shriek. Thank God, she doesn't have a camera, I think.

The mud-covered blonde walks into the little room next to the mud baths and is assaulted by a stream of water from a fire hose. The blast is so powerful it presses her against the wall and blasts away at her skin, probably taking off a layer of epithelium.

This is not the European manner, I think. This is more Slavic/Mongolian style. When the blonde recovers from the water attack, two thick matrons in white uniforms come over and scrub her with brushes. I begin to wonder if maybe Ivan hasn't created more of a Siberian/Gulag experience than a European emporium.

The attendant, who looks like a prison guard in a woman-behind-bars movie comes over to us. Obviously they have selected these women on the basis of the thickness and squatness of their bodies. This attendant, whose name tag reads Ludmilla in Cyrillic letters, orders us to get out of the mud and go for a rinse. Having witnessed the rinse, I let Barb go first. As she heads out, I notice a swimming pool of nice clear water through another door, so I slide through it.

Before anyone can nyet me, I slip into the lovely water and painlessly dissolve my blue mud. It's not long before Ludmilla stands angrily above me and informs me that I have just dirtied the pool for everyone else. I say, "Whoops, sorry," and get out.

After some weird veggie masks for our faces and some polarity treatments, Barb and I make it to the hair salon. This actually is the place I fear the most. Ivan Ivanovitch comes over to us and studies our bones. Then he gives us basically the same spiel they give you in every beauty salon around the world. He tells us how beauty is an individualistic thing and how he's going to bring out our own unique beauty. He calls it our own "special look."

While he talks I look around the salon. Most of the women coming out of this place have platinum blond hair cut in a variation of the old kitchen bowl haircut. They also have practically no eyebrows. So I guess that's this year's "special look."

While Ivan's assistants go for gowns, I whisper to Barb, "Protect your eyebrows. Remember whatever they do to you today will have to go over back in Maine."

Ivan's assistants gown us, put us in chairs at opposite sides of the room, feed us caviar and force us to listen to Prokofiev. When his assistant Sasha, pretending not to understand English, approaches me with the eyebrow tweezers, I actually have to grab his hands to stop him. Naturally there is a big fuss when I decline the haircut. Apparently other women have refused the tweezers, but no one has ever declined the haircut.

Ivan Ivanovitch himself comes over to talk to me. I explain to him that as a child I was a victim of abuse, having been raised by an aunt who was a seamstress, and that as a result I have an unnatural fear of scissors. I tell him that I am in therapy for this and that I'm sure in the months to come I will be able to overcome my childhood phobias and get a haircut in his salon.

This seems to satisfy him, but he says I must have a shampoo, rinse, and style. I accept this because you have to put up with something in these places. By the time they get done with us, I look exactly the same as when

I came in, although probably a lot cleaner, while Barb has no eyebrows and a white gold bowl of a haircut. Fortunately she does not yet realize what an assault they have committed upon her person. I decide not to point it out to her. Better for that realization to come later.

Finally I am shown into McTeagues's wainscotted office which displays among other memorabilia, a ship in a bottle, a suit of armor and the Scottish coat of arms for his clan. McTeague, over six feet four inches tall, wearing a black cashmere sweater and gray Baldessarini trousers, stands behind his desk. He has a fierce Scottish face framed by shoulder-length red hair that accentuates his most dominant feature; the bulging eyeballs of a hyperthyroid. "Molly Malone, you wanted to see me and here I am," he speaks in a big commanding voice overlaid with a brogue sounding a lot like Sean Connery. "Have you seen Ivan?"

Obviously he is confused because I still have my eyebrows and my hair is not platinum. I ignore his question and ask one of my own. "What's your connection to Ivan?"

"Very good friends." McTeague entwines his two fingers together to illustrate the point. "Ivan arrived penniless from Odessa," McTeague tells me. "The blackmarketeers had stripped him of his savings. He was sick. I nursed him back to health and set him up in this shop."

"How long have you worked in public relations?" I ask.

McTeague raises his eyebrows as if nobody ever asks him these questions. "Just a year or two. Before that I did nails. But let's cut to the chase. I'm the best in the business and I'm very expensive. I'm an animal, I have absolutely no standards, and everybody wants me. So the question really is, whether I want you?"

I can tell from the look in his eyes that he's bluffing. What publicity agent wouldn't be interested in a joint Stallone/Schwarzenegger production? But I allow him to play hard to get as we spend the better part of an hour going over the project. McTeague is virtually salivating over the tie-ins. He feels they're the key to the entire hype. The major thrust of his campaign as he sees it is to top the last great hype. McTeague explains as he paces hyperthyroidically back and forth, how tie-ins with Burger King, Pepsi, sleeping bags, mugs, bedspreads, paint, Fanny Farmer chocolates, bubble bath, lip balm, puzzles, flashlights, 3-D Viewmasters, chewing gum, coloring books, lunch bags, backpacks, Nintendo, Sega Genesis, sheets, towels, soap, pencils, pens, crayons, markers, perfume, and Etch-A-Sketch are simply not enough.

I settle back in my chair. This is the kind of talk I could get used to but unfortunately the conversation is over too soon and I am escorted out by one of Ivan's assistants. I stop to use the phone in the main salon to call Snake. I'm only on the phone for a minute when a strange woman approaches me. The woman, looking like something from Star Trek, is naked, except for a covering of green slimy leaves and I realize that she must be having the South China Seaweed Wrap. Even though she is dripping green vegetable slime all over the faux marble floor, the woman eyes me with annoyance as she waits to use the phone. She looks vaguely familiar and I think I should recognize her but I don't. I turn sideways from her to finish my call and that's when she attacks me.

Chapter Twenty-Two

I live through the attack. There were no weapons handy and the creature/ woman couldn't hit me with the telephone because I was holding it, nor could she rake me with her nails because they were wrapped in giant ocean fanweed. I suppose it must have looked like that B movie, Attack of the Swamp Woman or maybe a one woman mud wrestling match. But all my assailant could actually do was push and shove me, and jump on top of me, and that's when the big white coated attendants pull her off.

The most impressive thing about the whole attack actually is the woman's voice. She screams a threatening primal moan like a wounded bear defending her cubs as she curses and growls at me, and yells "Cheat - cheater."

The only damage I sustain is that I get a little slime on my tee shirt. While the weed woman has her seaweed wrap disturbed leaving big white gaps of flesh exposed. It's these facial gaps in her oceanic weed wrap that allow me to recognize - Wendy Kroy!

It doesn't occur to me until I'm out of the salon and on the way home with Barb that Wendy was probably there to see McTeague. and my getting to him before her must have enraged Wendy beyond the limits of her control. I can understand competition and anger. But I don't understand the mental device which allows her to see me as the "cheater" or thief, when it is actually she who's trying to steal from me. As Snake drives us home I wonder what other behavior Wendy can justify, since physical violence is obviously okay.

Because of Barb's visit, I have to spend a certain amount of time with her, mostly shopping. However when you add this to my already full schedule of morning conferences with Sly, twice a day lifting with Eric, aerobics with Mary Pat Johannsen, and T'ai chi on ice with Candy and the girls, my writing production falls off.

Hoping to speed my forward momentum, specifically my actual page production, I ask Snake to book me into some kind of commercial course on plotting. Unfortunately Truby's 22 Step Story course is already filled, so Snake signs me up instead for Truby's course on the Love Story. Artistically, I'm not interested in love stories. In fact, they have always bored me. I do have a romantic subplot in my action saga, but Sly has told me it will have to remain unresolved because of the heavy demands of the big action ending. And besides John Truby keeps saying weird stuff such as most love stories deal with the beginning of love while in reality we should be dealing with the renewal of love. And who the hell is going to risk writing something like that?

But I do believe I'm having a bit of a problem, and since it is a writing course I decide to listen and learn whatever I can to improve this small romantic subplot. The first thing I discover is that your heroine and your hero must be attractive. Now that's easy on film but way trickier in prose. For instance in every romance I have read, the hero is always described in some heart stopping manner which involves comparing his physiology to the glories of nature or the wonders of the universe. I know I am not capable of this.

Still I have to find a way to describe a male character in a way that is physically attractive to the reader. I listen to Truby do the Love Course and try to remember back to the last time I thought a man was physically attractive. Oh, I'm not talking about watching a Brad Pitt movie. I'm talking attractive as in you want to go to bed with the guy, as in you'll die if you can't have him. So I try to remember back to being in love with Dash. This is impossible. I have absolutely no recall of ever finding him remotely attractive. In fact our joint mutual history together is a complete mystery to me.

But I keep trying. Hair, I think, focus on Hair. All these romances obsess on hair because in the words of Vidal Sassoon, "Hair is Sex." So I sit in the room looking at the back of people's heads and how the light coming through the window plays on the various colors in their hair. I try hard to remember what color hair Dash has. Oh I know it's brown of course. But anyone who's ever read a romance, knows that no one's hair is just brown, there's golden brown, red brown, chestnut brown, chocolate brown, wheat brown, etc, etc. Unfortunately I have no recognition whatsoever of the nuances of shade in Dash's hair.

After several weeks of this concentration on romance, I'm always happy to get back home, sit around the pool and jaw with Sylvester. "So how's it going?" he asks.

I take a sip of my enzyme branching protein drink and say, "Great." I don't tell him the truth, which is that I spent some time today surfing the Net and playing with the shredder, and that despite all my best efforts, despite my spotless attendance record at the writing course, when I sat down at my computer this morning I couldn't come up with even one new sentence that I could stand to keep. Nor do I admit that it's gone beyond a slow down and that my worst fear has become real - I'm blocked.

I try to cheer myself with the thought that I've never had a writing block before. But it's also true that I've never been called upon to perform in such a high stakes game. And while I feel bad about not telling Sylvester that I'm nowhere near the end of my epic and that actually I'm not even really writing, I also cannot bring myself to do it.

"We've got a little shortfall in the financing of the film," Sly tells me.

Whenever he brings up anything regarding the pre-production activities for the film version of <u>Marga, Amazon Detective</u> my brain glazes over. Since I can't focus on the story I'm writing, how can I focus on the movie coming off the book.

"It's a gap but we'll work it out. You want to play some tennis?"

"I don't know, who're you playing with?"

"Arnold and Betsey."

"That blonde from the think tank?"

"She's the Chairman now."

Sylvester has been spending alot of time with this long legged blonde who is supposed to have a higher recorded I.Q. than Marilyn vos Savant. I give him a look. "I don't like her laugh. It's really a giggle."

Sylvester departs and I go back to another unproductive stretch in front of my computer screen, then head out for a lifting session with Eric. Every time I see Eric, I realize he's so strange that I really should look for another trainer, but my mind is just too occupied to add one more thing so I guess I've decided to treat him like a piece of furniture - like a chair with a wobbly leg.

Eric and I have such a set routine by now, that we usually start our workout in silence. I mean we don't even say hello. We both wear body clothes (okay so I now wear spandex to lift but it is black) and we settle into a series of lifting and spotting that is like a slow familiar dance.

After about twenty minutes we usually talk a bit and I tell Eric today about McTeague's concept of market seeding. "It's the precurser to hype," I explain. "Hype tells the audience what's available but seeding makes them want the product even before it arrives."

"Great."

"And McTeague says that my novel isn't the market product, It's the Marga character that's the product because it can be delivered in so many different forms like dolls, jewelry, colorforms, games, perfume."

"What did you say the guy's name was?"

"McTeague."

Eric repeats the name to himself as if he will forget it without the repetition. "And you're hiring this guy?"

"Yeah," I say casually. "He's also making up a clothing and jewelry line for me. The clothes are a little ultra, one shoulder skins things like Tina Turner wore in Thunderdome. You know cute in sort of a Sheena, Queen of the Jungle way, so I sent his designers back to the drawing board on that one. But the jewelry's not bad. Look at this." I shake my head to show off my bone earrings.

Eric touches them carefully like they're really delicate and might break or something. "Are these made of human bone?"

God, he's stupid, I think but just answer "No," without saying they're plastic and made in Taiwan.

"Well ...I drove somebody yesterday."

"Who?" I ask even though I don't care. Just about the only thing Eric ever has to talk about is the importance of the party he chauffeured.

While Eric and I talk, we move around each other, taking different positions in regard to the machinery and the weights as well as each other, getting a little sweaty.

I take a look at myself in the mirror as we move about the room. I am beginning to see the development of muscle on my body. Oh it's nothing dramaticly big or chunky, but when I do my arm work, for the first time I can see the muscle cuts and my legs which have always been okay, look really nice. I don't know why but the muscular definition does makes my body look more sensual.

While I am thinking this, an uninvited male walks into the gym, interrupting Eric and me in the middle of power training - the male is uninvited but familiar - it's Dash.

"Who let him in here?" I demand.

"I did," Arnold admits stepping inside. "He said he was your husband."

"Oh yeah," is all I can think of to say.

"Is there a problem?" Arnold asks.

"Uh-oh," Eric gathers up his belongings, stuffs them in his gym bag and leaves.

"I want him out of here." I point to Dash figuring this should present no difficulty for Arnold who can throw anybody out of anywhere.

But Arnold frowns the Teutonic frown. "He said he's your husband and the father of your children."

"That's why I want him out of here."

Arnold shakes his head from side to side. "I don't get it." I'd like to tell Arnold to go back to something easy like cold fusion, but I don't. Meanwhile, Dash sticks out his hand and introduces himself. Arnold smiles his big gap-toothed grin and engages Dash in a conversation on how the construction business is temporarily floundering around L.A. but how the ice rink building business is flourishing ever since "Wayne the Great One" came to town and how everybody wants an ice rink in the back yard, including Arnold. "Did you know that woman's hockey will be included in the next Winter Olympics?"

Oh no, I think, feeling miserable. I know this talk, this is jock talk. And there is no cement on earth that bonds faster and firmer than jock talk. Before I know it, Dash is asking Arnold about his experiences as President Bush's physical fitness counselor and Arnold is asking Dash for advice on the best ice skating training methods for children.

I clear my throat. They don't even notice. I make a show of gathering up my gym stuff in preparation for stalking out. Still nothing. I begin to walk away. They look over, wave and continue talking... something about Dash building a rink in Arnold's back yard.

This is a nightmare.

Chapter Twenty-Three

Mortified and mesmerized I sit down to read - starting with the synopsis which explains that Marga the Amazon detective who comes from an isolated clan of Amazons who have survived in isolation for several centuries, has been captured by slavers and sold on the auction block in Ancient Rome. However, by saving the life of her master, she is released from her bonds of slavery and allowed to live as a freewoman and make her living as a private detective in the degenerating city. One day, Marga is summoned by the Governor of Galatia to find his runaway wife, who's name is Valentina Vesuvia.

Of course I get madder and madder as I read. I guess when they steal in L.A., they don't even bother to change the names of the characters. I rush to read further. Since Wendy has stolen both my premise and my characters and the manuscript is 650 pages, I have to wonder how she's developed my story.

In my impatience, I begin flipping through large segments, looking for the kinds of complications you expect to find in the middle of a story, but instead I find a long segment on the nutrition of the average Roman citizen and then another on how water was carried via high acqueducts (actually this appears to be word-for-word my own discarded prose.) When on impulse, I flip to the end, I find not a real ending, but one of those phony non-endings where Marga just packs up her rabbit skin duffel and prepares to go home.

I read more and more, faster and faster, until finally I decide that Wendy Kroy has ghosted just exactly and precisely what she stole from me. While nothing of mine has been left unplundered, it's also clear that no one has developed the story, someone just filled it out and puffed it up.

At this point, the phone starts ringing. I listen to my answering machine take messages from Elliot Stanton and McTeague, and then one from Snake who requests that I meet with Sly and Arnold at the pool in thirty minutes.

I know that I have to talk to the guys and the sooner the better but I'm so nervous I can't sit still and there are goosebumps all over my arms. So I slip into the pool and engage in furious laps of the Australian crawl. When I make my speed turn at poolside, Sly taps me on the head, so I crawl out of the pool and drip onto the mosaic tile.

I can tell with a glance that both Sly and Arnold have read the rip off. It's dusk and the fading sunlight filters through the rattling giant fan palms beside the pool. We sit at the big table on top of which they have placed some kind of legal document. As if I'm not nervous enough -

Sly looks more serious than I have ever seen him before. He asks me if I have been using the paper shredder and locking up my computer disks in the safe every night, as he previously instructed me. I assure him that I have been doing that. Then he and Arnold take turns solemnly relating the calls they have received from Wendy Kroy since the delivery of her manuscript. Wendy told them that she has three of the fastest ghost writers in the country on her payroll, as well as a specialist on anthropology and Ancient Roman history. She also asked them what kind of visuals and ending they want, because she plans to tailor the work to their specifications and deliver it complete ... within 48 hours!

I listen to all this with a sinking heart. Ever since I arrived here I've felt like I was on some merry adventure, the outcome of which didn't matter. But the truth is, that the longer I've been here, the more I've realized that the heroine I've created is the best part of me. And my hope of success (due to the participation of Sly and Arnold) has grown to the point that I have come to feel that this success is really mine - it belongs to me. This expectation has given me my major reason for getting up in the morning. Oh sure, I've pretended that my adventure has been some kind of crazy Alice-in-Wonderland/Gail Sheehy/mid-life crisis, but I'm keenly aware that this is my life that's in the balance.

The details of failure; having to leave my writing studio in Guest House Number Three - packing Victor for the long bitter drive back East - the idea of returning to my previous family life as a failure, or the alternative, clerking at a bookstore (which is the only real life job for which I am truly suited) seems worse than death. Better I think, to drive Victor and myself off one of those cliffs on Route 1. That would at least put a tragic Southern California/Joan Didion/Sylvia Plath end to me.

I try to remember what Sly and Arnold have taught me especially the part about how to behave in a crisis. I remember I'm supposed to be strong, believe in myself, and maintain my focus and drive in the face of hostile forces. In short, play my game. I summon up the very last little remnant of my nerve. My voice comes out scratchy, but I manage, "I still think I can do a better job than Wendy Kroy."

Sly and Arnold smile, "So do we." Then they tell me that they both feel that the work submitted by Wendy Kroy was puffed and stuffed, and that Wendy's ghosts may be fast but they lacked an essential quality which they both agree all of my writing displays in abundance - heart.

"Furthermore," Sly continues, "we want you to know that we have such complete confidence in you," Sly pauses here for effect while Arnold smiles, "that we've decided to personally fund the shortfall in the financing and ... we both want to star as your gladiator sidekicks."

This just blows me away - that they are both willing to risk their money and reputations on me. I put my arms around these two. I have to reach up to do it, and my arms aren't long enough to get around the shoulders of Stallone and Schwarzenegger, but I do the best I can. I rub my Golden Knot of Hercules and hold it up to the fading sunlight. I look at the same golden knot around their massive necks. "I love you guys, you know." Sly's eyes get a little misty and Arnold looks like he's in the last quarter of a winning football game. It's a special moment until Arnold opens up the legal contract. "The lawyers say you just have to sign this,"

"Okay," I swallow. "What does it say?'

Arnold shrugs. "It's just the usual production and delivery deadlines and guarantees - script approval, trailers, final cut."

The word 'deadline' really gives me a chill, because it makes me remember that I'm only on page 117 of my 600 page saga. How can I sign anything when I still have no finished product? How can I make any kind of agreement in which I have to deliver what I've promised - <u>on deadline</u>? I mean I know I can deliver, but like Margaret Mitchell's, <u>Gone with the Wind</u>, it might take ten years. Who can be sure?

"What are the deadlines?" I ask.

"Three months for the book and three months for the script which seems fair." I guess it seems fair to them since they think I'm near the end. I'm so shook up by this that when Arnold hands me the legal papers, I fumble and the legal contract falls to the ground and begins skittering along the imported tile. Before I can retrieve it, it has fluttered into the pool.

"I'm sorry," I tell Arnold and Sylvester and this is true. I am sorry for drying up, for getting blocked, for deceiving my two friends and for not even having the guts to admit it.

"That's okay Moll," Sylvester days. "We'll just get another copy and leave it in your studio. But obviously you've got a major leakage problem here, and we don't want another incident like this with Kroy. If she makes another attempt to steal your story and she gets it in more complete form, she won't be able to get anywhere with us but maybe she'll be able to get something cooking with some other producers. So you'd better find the leak and plug it."

Over the next few days, I believe that my turn to paranoia is entirely reasonable. After all Wendy Kroy didn't just steal all my characters, even down to the correct spelling of their names but she even lifted certain sections word-for-word. So clearly this theft was an inside job and she must have used someone who had easy access to the compound, someone who could come and go anywhere in the estate, especially my writing studio ...someone I trusted. The possibilities flicker through my mind, and with each face I try to remember back to any unusual circumstances - Snake? Lucky? Nick? Vinnie? Trip? Eric? Lips? Beverly Hills is just another small town where everybody knows everybody else. It could be any of them. This is like a bad dream.

Needless to say, I'm not in a great mood, when I come into my next session with Eric. Wordlessly we begin lifting, our bodies working together in a kind of ballet of lifting and spotting, communicating physically but not verbally until we're wet with sweat. And for the first time (I can be a little dense about some things) I realize that there is an erotic quality to our training. When Eric pulls off his wet shirt and reaches into his gym bag to pull out a dry one, he also pulls out a big brown bottle. "I think I'm going to paint you today," he says.

He's got to be kidding. "Is that the stuff that makes all the women lifters look like roasted turkeys?" I laugh.

"Molly you know that muscle definition shows up better on dark skin."

"Maybe, but I have no intention of using that stuff."

Eric scrunches up his face as if it has never occurred to him that I might refuse. "I'm the trainer, you're the client," he says trying to gain some authority over me.

Yeah, right. As if after what I've been through, the face-to-face confrontation with Sly and Arnold, the detailed contemplation of imminent failure, and the emotional exhaustion that followed, there's not a chance in the world that Eric could ever influence me to do anything. But Eric thinks some more. He's the kind of person that you can actually watch while he thinks. Obviously it's important to him that I be painted and he thinks that if he can just find the right way to communicate the importance of this to me, then I will agree. "Molly," he says after a tortured thinking kind of pause, "You know how I told you that Rachel McLish is almost perfect."

"Yeah?"

"Well I think you have become completely perfect...and I know that this will become even more apparent to everyone when you have been painted a darker color."

There is something in the way those handsome blue eyes look at me that gives me the creeps. He makes it worse by saying. "I also want you to know that I think you are the most special person I have ever driven. And I just want to be around you...all the time."

Even though I'm tired, even though I've been through an emotional hurricane, I realize at this point that Eric represents a different kind of danger. In fact maybe Eric has gone a little nuts.

"Well Eric," I smile at him, "You really are around me all the time, aren't you? I mean I'll bet I spend more total time with you than I spend with anyone."

But that's not good enough for Eric. "You don't understand," he whispers. "I don't just want to be around you...all the time. I need to be around you ...all the time."

Chapter Twenty-Four

So I can't write and I'm exhausted because I can't sleep. I must have insomnia because I'm up all night creeping around my bungalow trying to figure out who the thief is. I pace back and forth reviewing possible suspects and wringing my hands. I wonder if maybe I'm having a breakdown. With so much on my mind I feel so disconnected that I think about not showing up for the midnight session of T'ai chi on ice at Candy's. But I make myself go, thinking that a break from worrying might help, but unfortunately it doesn't.

Afterwards, as I sit quietly at Candy's pool, drinking a margarita from a little green cactus shaped glass with my circle of sisters; Candy, Mary Pat, Lips, and Barb, I don't wisecrack as much as usual and they notice. "What the hell is wrong with you?" Barb asks.

I roll my eyes, I mean, there's so many topics to choose from, I decide to start with something small. "Well I'm having a problem with my trainer. I think he might be stalking me."

"You should talk that over with Sly," Candy tells me. "He knows all about stalking."

"I think Molly's got something else on her mind." Lips suggests. "She looks like she's in deep thought."

"What's to think about?" Barb demands, as always the pragmatist. Life to Barb is the sum total of the decisions: What am I wearing? and Where's my next vacation? The reason she respects Candy so much is that Candy always has the answers to those question. Actually Candy seems to have the answers to all questions.

That's why I decide to bring up my most serious problem - my security problem. I'm thinking that if I use the group as a sounding board and run through my list of possible suspects, maybe they can help me figure out who's stealing my material. But when I open my mouth to start this discussion, a completely different question just slides out of my mouth, "I was wondering...Do you think a person can ever really change?"

Candy refills her little green glass from the ever present jug of margaritas. This is a sign of interest. "What kind of change?"

"I'm talking about a real change, a basic change in personality."

Mary Pat sips her drink and checks her eye makeup with a little mirror from her purse. "Well, you know me, I believe in miracles."

Yeah, we know. The intense strong-hearted goodness and optimism Mary Pat has always shown in the face of degeneration, meanness, ankle biting and all the lesser forms of evil common to every day life, has astonished us all. I think we'd all like her to walk in bitchy one day with a really good case of greed or envy so we could verbally slap her around a bit.

Then Barb asks, "You're talking about Dash?"

"Well..."

"Yes, you are so talking about Dash," she accuses me. "And my advice to you is to take him back. From what I've seen you've scared him into submission and he'll be good for the rest of his life. Forget about changing him - scared is always better than changed."

"He is behaving better," I admit, "but something is missing."

"The only thing missing is that before he used to wet on the floor and now he's housebroken."

I shake my head. "That's not it. The problem is something basic, something chemical is gone." And this may be the big truth I haven't wanted to admit. Every time I think about Dash, it's always in a logical, detached, what's-the-best-thing-to-do modality. Never once have I felt any emotion and I think that's what's bothering me. "I just don't have any feelings left for him," I tell my friends, stating this simple truth out loud for the first time.

"What are you talking about?" Barb asks.

Lips stirs the jug and pours herself a drink. "She's talking about love."

"Give me a break."

"Don't you care about love?" Lips asks.

123

"I figure out what I want," Barb studies her manicure. "I figure out how to get it. When I get it, then I'm happy."

Candy touches my arm. "You know Molly you may be suffering from a depression due to a sudden loss of phenylethylamine. Maybe you need to eat chocolate which is loaded with phenylethylamine." Candy always holds court at the pool. No one questions her, not even Barb. And that is because Candy has married a man richer than Barb's and has therefore proved her greater intelligence, knowledge, and reliability.

"I think it has more to do with that liquid chlorophyll diet that Eric has me on."

"Or... your problem could be pheromonal," Candy adds.

"Beg your pardon?" Mary Pat says.

"Well, you know all sexual attraction in animals is controlled by pheromones, airborne chemical substances. And this French scientist has just discovered a receptor inside the human nose. He's calling it the vomeronasal receptor. So the latest scientific theory is that we may think we're making relationship or psychological decisions about the opposite sex, but actually we're controlled by these pheromones."

Lips ponders that. "Wow! So Molly might have a clogged nose?"

"Exactly," Candy says. "Something may have happened to her biochemically that hampers her ability to pick up Dash's scent."

I wonder what to make of this because it is true that I have a few allergies and have always had a poor sense of smell, but nothing has happened to me. It's not like I've been hit in the face with a door or something.

But Mary Pat is nodding her head emphatically. "That would explain why Chuck Jones became so obsessed with Marla Maples Trump's shoes. You know these shoe fetish people love the shoe even more than the person. Maybe it's because they sniff the scent from the inside of the shoe. And it's not the person they love, it's the scent."

"It also explains the menstrual synchrony in women who are in close contact with one another," Candy suggests, "and how blindfolded mothers can identify their infants. Did you realize that it's been scientifically proven that the timing of a woman's menstruation can be altered by smearing her upper lip with an extract of male underarm sweat? Did you know they're actually making a pheromonal perfume?"

Barb, who seemed bored up to this point, is now interested. "No kidding? Where do you get it?"

"I don't know," Candy says. "Some French guy is working on it. Maybe you have to go to France to get it."

Barb looks sulky. "Figures."

Mary Pat clears her throat. "Molly, do you want to try to get back together with Dash? Is that what you're thinking?" It's obvious that Mary Pat has slipped into her consoler/counselor thing.

"I think it would be best for the children."

"But would it be best for you?" Barb asks.

"I don't know. Maybe...if I could actually get my heart in it."

Mary Pat rearranges her towel. "So what do you see when you look at him?"

"I don't know. I don't think I really look at him anymore."

"Ah!" Candy murmurs. "Elie Weisel says the opposite of love is not hate. It's apathy."

Barb raises her hands in a gesture of leadership. "Okay, let's just be analytical and cold about this for a minute. Molly, what would you say are Dash's good qualities?"

I shrug. "Well he's good looking."

Barb shakes her head. "That doesn't count in a husband."

"He's funny," I offer.

"That also doesn't count in a husband."

Now I have to think. "He likes to work. He's good in bed."

"That counts," they all nod at this. Barb continues to prompt me, "What else?"

"He loves the boys..." I don't know. What do you say about a husband? He's never hit me, he's not a drunk, he's not a cheater." I realize however, that these are not positive qualities, just the absence of negatives.

Lips has her pouty lips pursed together in disdain. "Is this some kind of magazine quiz, Barb? I mean are you going to rate her answers or something?"

Barb ignores her. Ever since she learned that Lips paid off part of Snake's car loan, she lost the little respect she had for her.

Candy studies her fingernails, "Molly, when you're standing next to Dash, exactly what do you feel?"

"Nothing."

"Well, my feelings are very vivid," Candy says. "When I'm standing next to a man, I always feel something. Although in your case, it certainly sounds like it could be a clogged vomernoasal receptor."

"So what should she do?" Barb asks. "See a nose doctor?"

"I don't know," Candy admits.

Lips finishes her drink and pours another. "I don't really buy this stuff. I myself have always just looked at the light."

"What light?" Candy asks.

"The light around people."

Barb narrows her eyes. She will listen to any of Candy's theories, but Lips has not proven herself in the financial aspects of the romance market and therefore in Barb's opinion is not allowed to express an opinion. "Is this going to be a New Age thing?" Barb asks haughtily.

"You know how there's that light around Sylvester?" Lips continues.

"I've seen that light," I agree. "It's easiest to see when Sly is wearing black silk and the sun is behind him. I've seen a little light around Arnold too,"

Lips nods emphatically. "My theory is that most people use up all their energy just looking out for themselves. Then they don't have anything left over for anybody else. But some people have so much energy that they can take care of themselves and also have some energy to give to you and me. And that's why those people have a light around them."

Candy tilts her head. "Are we talking auras, or is this an energy field theory?"

"I don't analyze it scientifically," Lips admits. "I just use it."

"And how exactly do you use this light theory?" Barb asks, barely hiding her skepticism.

"When I want to know what kind of person I'm dealing with, in terms of ...well goodness, niceness you know, I just throw my eyes out of focus a little and look to see if they're throwing any light."

"Well, that's interesting," I murmur. I definitely like it better than the clogged nose theory. But I wonder why I brought up Dash anyway. What temporary insanity came over me? I was going to talk about my security problem. I was going to talk about how to find the thief and how to plug the leak.

I pour another round of Margaritas for the gals and take advantage of the temporary lull in the conversation to outline my security problem to the group. Because of the technical aspects of the problem, Mary Pat, Barb and Lips tune right out. But Candy listens carefully to my descriptions of how I handle my computer disks and papers, in addition to my detailed suspicions of certain individuals (leaving out anyone present, of course) as well as my analysis of most likely culprits based on opportunity and inclination.

When I finally give her a chance, she asks, "Do you have a fax/modem hooked up to your computer?"

"Yes."

"Are you set up so that material can be sent directly to your computer? In other words, can other computers communicate with your machine directly?"

"Well, sure all my research requests are reported back to the computer, and I do get e-mail."

Candy frowns, "I think an experienced hacker has broken into your computer system by telephone via the modem. You may never know exactly who the thief is, but you can shut the door."

"That's what I have to do, shut the door... plug the leak."

"Okay, then call Atlas Security, ask for Clarence Chen and tell him you need to have your computer encrypted."

"That's it?"

"It was an easy question," Candy sips daintily from her little cactus shaped glass. "The husband question was a lot harder."

Chapter Twenty-Five

I wake up in the back of the limo, duct tape around my wrists, around my ankles, and tape over my mouth. I manage to swing my legs over the seat and sit up.

My God, we're on the Santa Monica Freeway! Jaguars and Lamborghini's and Range Rovers crowd the traffic lanes next to us but nobody notices me. I'm side by side with them in traffic, duct tape over my mouth, and they don't even see me. They're all busy on their cellular phones, or listening to music. Eric speaks to me over the intercom.

"You're thinking that maybe you can smash the window glass in order to get somebody's attention," he says. "Well, forget it."

I can't answer because of the duct tape over my mouth.

"Remember Molly the glass is tinted and bullet proof. You're locked in and no one can see you. If you think this through, I believe you'll come to the conclusion that it's wasted effort to resist me."

I think about this for a while and he does seem to be right.

"Now I'm prepared to remove all the duct tape if you promise you won't make trouble or do anything to call attention to us. Blink twice if your answer is yes."

I blink twice.

Eric drives a little way and then has to stop because we're stuck in traffic. He motors down the window between the driver and passenger compartment, pulls a small knife out of his pocket and cuts the tape away from my wrists and ankles. But when he pulls the duct tape off my mouth I can't help but give an involuntary scream. God, that hurt! Whatever invisible facial hairs lived above my lip are gone forever now.

"Quiet!" Eric warns me.

"Sorry."

When the traffic eases up a bit and Eric puts the limo in drive, I try to assess my situation. Actually there's not much to think about. I'm kidnapped, Eric is in charge, and I don't have any ideas. In the past, I have found that the usual reason for not having an idea is lack of research, so I ask, "Is this a traditional kidnapping for ransom or is it one of these psychotic things where you have to possess me?" I do wonder if this is a sex thing because of the way Eric's been looking at me for the past few weeks.

"I just want to drive you around."

"That's it?"

"Yeah." Eric motors the window between us back up into place. I settle back in the leather seat and look around the passenger compartment. There's a phone in the center console. I pick it up and punch in 911. "I turned off the outgoing," Eric tells me over the intercom.

I slip the phone back into place and look around some more. There's a fax machine built into the console and although I think Eric probably disconnected that too, I turn on the power and the little green light does come on. I can communicate with the fax just as well as the phone, if I just had some paper to write on - or a computer.

I look out the window. Everybody else is talking on their phone. It's so unfair that I don't have a phone. Then I get an idea. Pressing the intercom button, I say, "Oh Eric," in my best mistress-to-servant tone of voice. "I believe I was carrying my laptop when you abducted me."

"Yes."

"Well as long as I'm going to be stuck back here, I'd like to get some work done," I say, trying for a Bette Davis voice.

Eric lowers the window between us and hands me my laptop. "Are you actually going to write while I'm driving you around?"

"Yes Eric, that's my plan, so would you put the window back up so I can concentrate?"

"Sure." He motors the window back up.

I plug the lap top into the fax and type:

Urgent Memo:
To Sylvester Stallone:

Sly, I have been kidnapped by Wicked Eric - He is driving East on the Santa Monica Freeway. Please advise.

I am gratified to receive a fast answer.

Memo:
From the office of Sylvester Stallone:
Molly, thank you for your communication. This matter will be attended to immediately.

That's when I know that Sylvester is beyond of the reach of his office. Otherwise he would have answered himself. It's a few minutes before Eric's phone rings and when I pick up the extension in the back, I hear Snake's voice. "Cmon Eric," he says. "You know you can't do this kind of thing."

"I just want to drive her around," Eric insists.

"Yeah sure but you've already done that, so now bring her home."

"No."

I decide to break in, "Where's Sly?"

"He's playing polo," Snake says.

"Well interrupt his game."

"Mr. Stallone doesn't like to be called off the field." I can't believe this. Snake tries again with Eric, "All right how much do you want?"

"You think this is about money?" Eric sounds insulted. "Money has nothing to do with this. I'm going to drive Molly to my garage and paint her."

"Before you said you were just going to drive her around. Now you're saying you're going to take her to your garage and paint her. What else are you planning to do?"

Eric hangs up on him and then he disconnects my fax. Thinking that I may be stuck here for some time, I decide to adopt a cordial, gracious, victim-to-kidnapper attitude and Eric responds well to this. When I tell him I'm hungry, he orders us some Happy Family from the Chinese takeout place on Wilshire.

While we're driving over there, the phone rings again and I listen in on the the extension. "Eric, what the hell do you think you're doing?"

It's Sylvester, he sounds angry, and I think I hear Arnold's voice in the background. "Bring her back here."

"I can't. I have to paint her."

"Why?"

"Sly...you know how hard it is to see muscle definition when the skin is pale. I have a new paint that I've mixed up myself and it'll be perfect on her because it's got more gold in it than bronze."

There is a pause. "Look Eric you've cracked up. You realize that don't you? But there's still time to bring Molly back home. We haven't called the police into this yet."

I shriek into the phone, "You haven't called the police?"

"Is that you Molly?" Sly asks. "The publicity people don't want us to do anything to jeopardize the film and it sounds like you're pretty much okay for now so we're going to negotiate."

"I can't believe you would call the police on me," Eric sounds surprised.

"Well what did you think was going to happen?'

"I thought we would put friendship and art above commerce. But fine, fine, if you're going to be that way about it ..." Eric is beginning to sound a little pouty, "then I want fifty thousand dollars. I'm not bringing her back until I get fifty thousand dollars."

Gee, he could have asked for more, I think. I mean fifty thousand isn't a lot for a ransom.

"How'd you arrive at that figure? Sly asks.

"...Why?"

"Well... I know what my lawyer's gonna say. First thing he's gonna say is, Sly can we do this for less?"

I'm thinking I can't be hearing this right. I'm thinking that Sly could not possibly be bargaining me down.

"Well you just go right ahead and talk to your lawyer," Eric tells him stubbornly."

It is at this moment that Eric's words 'mixed up myself' suddenly connect for me. "Hey wait a minute, Eric, what's in that paint?" But he won't answer. "Eric, remember that James Bond movie where the villain paints the girl with real gold and she dies because her skin can't breathe? What about that, Eric?"

He still won't answer. I don't believe this. Hasn't everyone's seen Goldfinger? Meanwhile I realize that I haven't considered the most important thing - if Eric's obsessed with painting me, what else is he obsessed with? I mean, what if he has plans for my stuffed and painted torso to be mounted on the wall of his garage apartment?

I hear Sylvester's loud exhale of frustration and then the muffled sound of Sly and Arnold conferencing in the background. Finally Arnold's voice comes confidentially over the line. "Don't worry, Eric. Everything's going to be all right. Even as we speak, we've got the accountants on the other phone line and we're working this out."

"What's the problem?" Eric asks.

"Taxes, we have to decide which account we're going to take the money from. Did Molly tell you we're into pre-production with the film?"

"Yeah."

"Well, Eric, I'm sure you understand that we'd like to categorize this as a pre-production expense because then we can deduct it. However if the accountants say no, then Sly and I will pay you personally. My lawyers will talk to his lawyers and we'll hammer something out. So whatever you do, don't worry."

But there's another voice in the background, a lot less soothing than Arnold. And it takes me a moment before I recognize the sound of Dash yelling, "What do you mean? Molly's being driven around by some maniac and nobody's called the police?!"

Eric sighs, shrugs his shoulders, then pulls into the Chinese place and parks. He locks me in the limo while he gets the take out and I do have to marvel while he's in there, at how completely Eric has isolated me from the rest of the world. And he doesn't even have a hideout...all he has is a car. His technique could revolutionalize and streamline the criminal art of kidnapping.

I'm thinking about this, almost admiring Eric's sick ingenuity when another limo pulls up next to us. It's a long stretch in a fashionable gun metal gray color. The door opens and Wendy Kroy wearing a dark narrow dress, a black straw hat, and a long black and white silk scarf gets out and hurries into the Chinese place.

Chapter Twenty-Six

Holding big paper cartons of Happy Family, Wendy Kroy and Weird Eric come out together and I can tell from the body language that they are much friendlier than I ever imagined. Eric walks Wendy to her limo, hands her the cartons of Chinese food and waits while Wendy unties her long silk scarf and hands it to him, like it's a gift or something, and then Eric returns to me.

I guess I want to believe that Eric and Wendy's meeting is just an accident and that Eric is going to continue to drive me around while fantasizing about painting me like a roasted Thanksgiving turkey, but the first thing Eric does when he gets back in our car, is tie Wendy's scarf over my mouth, effectively gagging me. Then he wraps wide rubber exercise bands around my wrists and hobbles my feet together, which is aggravating to say the least but the gag is the biggest problem.

This puts me at a tremendous disadvantage since my mouth is probably the most effective part of my body. When I could talk to Eric I was sure I could manipulate his small reptilian brain. But without the ability to communicate, I think I'm in a much deeper hole than I previously thought.

The second thing Eric does when he gets back in the car, is to slide a pair of oversize sunglasses onto the bridge of my nose and throw a big hooded middle-eastern shawl over my head and shoulders. Then he opens the door and pushes me out of the back of our limo and into the back of Wendy's.

While he does this, Wendy's uniformed driver moves from Wendy's limo to the driver's seat of Eric's limo. Eric then gets behind the wheel of Wendy's stretch and pulls out of the parking lot. And I sit, tied and gagged and sunglassed in the back of Wendy Kroy's car while Eric drives. They talk for a long time, those two. It irritates me that I can't hear what they're saying because the plexiglass partition is up, but they seem to be having an intense discussion almost an argument, that ends finally in some kind of agreement and smiles. Meanwhile the car heads South.

We drive down Route # 101 and then cross to the 405. The landscape becomes drier and we see more rock, and cactus. I wonder what kind of deal those two have made. Eric is such a pawn and a weakling, that Wendy must definitely have dominated him. And if Wendy's in charge, I'm at a big disadvantage because she really hates me. It was clear from the beginning, when she tried to steal my detective idea, to her hacking into my computer, to her attack on me at Ivan's, but I guess I was too busy with my story to take much notice.

And where are we going? I have a bad feeling they're taking me to Mexico. Obviously something's on the drawing board because the ploy of sending Wendy's driver to Eric's limo was obviously designed to throw Sly and Arnold off our track. This gives me the shivers.

We drive for a long time without stopping. It's dead quiet in the back, and I doze off. I wake up when I feel the car come to a stop and see that Eric has pulled into a line to cross the border. A bored customs official speaks to Eric, and Eric hands him some papers. This is when I understand the cleverness of how they have disguised me. Because the black hooded shawl covers my gagged mouth and drapes over my shoulders covering my tied wrists. All I have left to communicate with is my eyes, and they are covered with sunglasses. It all works very well, the guard waves us through and we're in Mexico.

Leaning against the back seat I tell myself that I'll get another chance to escape but I wonder. In terms of kidnappers, Wendy seems much more organized and resourceful than Eric. Once over the border, we pass little pastel houses with tin roofs, and the signs advertising cervesa and gasolina but they grow sparser and we begin to enter a more barren, sterile, rocky region and I think we must be in the Baha. Driving down highway #1 we pass Ensenada and Punta Prieta. We see fewer and fewer signs of human habitation and the highway becomes a long black line with occasional red dirt roads leading off to either side. We see nobody, keep driving, and the sun sets.

Eventually just south of Santa Rosalia, Eric pulls off the main highway, onto a heavily rutted dirt road. With Wendy directing, he drives us past many small roads until eventually we take a right turn and pull into the driveway of a very tall wooden house with dark closed shutters and Eric turns off the car.

Wendy gets out to open up the house and Eric follows with a few duffel bags. He returns for me, removes the gag, and with his pocket knife he cuts the rubber bands so that I can walk. I'm stiff from sitting in one position for so long so he has to he help me up the two flights of stairs and into a large room with wide glass doors that lead out to a balcony. Outside the moon is very large and reflects upon the ocean which is either the Pacific or the Sea of Cortez. I'm not sure which, since I got disoriented during the drive. Eric deposits me in a chair and even thought the room is bright from the moonlight, he lights a several tall candles. "Where's the generator?" he asks Wendy, handing her back her scarf which she ties around her alligator purse.

"Don't bother with that now," she tells him.

I sit slumped in my chair, rubbing my sore wrists. It seems like forever since I had anything to eat, or drink and I ache all over from the confinement. Wendy leans in close to me and smiles, "Prison," she says. "You're going to a Mexican prison."

I don't say anything.

"Think about living in a small communal space with fifty or sixty women, and one working toilet. Forget taking a walk, forget seeing a doctor, forget reading newspapers, books, letters, and writing --- we're talking about a place where you might wait a year to get a pencil and then you won't have any paper." She laughs a loud snort like a horse. "Think about the heat...think about the bugs....the snakes....think about chronic diarrhea."

"But I haven't done anything."

"I'm going to make an anonymous call to the authorities, and they'll find you here with a nice assortment of illegal substances." She looks at Eric, "What have we got anyway?"

"A little weed, some coke, a bottle of downers."

Wendy looks satisfied. "That'll do."

"Nobody's going to believe such an obvious set-up," I say stalling for time.

"I'm a friend of the local Captain and I'm sure he'll believe it. Tie her back up," she tells Eric, "I'm going to make the phone call."

Eric rummages around in the kitchen cabinets, "Use the cell phone."

"No, I'll use a phone that can't be linked to us."

"People are looking for me," I tell Wendy before she leaves.

But she looks unconcerned, "Sly and Arnold can't help you when you're in a completely different country... and I have a feeling that somehow they'll find a way to make the movie without you." She heads for the stairs and then pauses at the top, "Maybe they'll even hire me to take your place."

I listen to her footsteps on the stairs and then the sound of the heavy front door closing behind her. Can this be it for me...to be left tied up for the Mexican police to drag away on a phony drug charge? I try so hard to think of a way out but I'm distracted by the sound of my own beating heart.

Eric must be out of tape and rubber, because he searches around in the kitchen cabinets for quite a while before finding a long piece of twine. Then he comes over and ties me to the chair. He doesn't bother to gag me but I guess there's no longer any need.

"What did Wendy promise you to get you to go along with this?" I ask him.

"My own fitness program...on cable, maybe network, but definitely at least on cable."

"When did you make this deal?"

"At the Chinese takeout place. Wendy's got one of these illegal monitoring devices that allows her to listen in on cell phone conversations and she was driving around listening in on stuff when she heard us. That's how she knew I had you in the car."

"Eric..." I wait until he looks me in the eye. "I'm sure I can make you a better offer than Wendy - maybe something in the movie? I know we can work this out because you're not even really in trouble yet."

He shakes his head, "Oh yes, I am. Kidnapping and fraud in two countries. Wendy already explained it to me and I think I'd better stick with the deal I made with her."

"But Eric...don't you still want to paint me?" I try to sound seductive with this.

He looks surprised. "Wendy said I couldn't."

"Why not? What difference could it possibly make if I'm wearing body paint when they cart me off to prison? Besides Wendy's not even here."

Eric looks at me like a sixteen year old boy, but then he frowns and shakes his head. "I don't think I still have the paint. I might have left it in the other limo."

"But you mixed that paint up yourself, maybe you can make up another mixture, there must be things around here you could use."

Eric doesn't answer me, but he frowns again like he's thinking this over. He goes back into the kitchen area and starts looking through cabinets. Soon he places glasses and bowls up on the counter, along with an assortment of liquids and begins mixing. Eventually Eric approaches me with a big bowl of brown liquid and a small dish towel.

He gets down on his knees, places the bowl on the floor, and looks up at me, "I'm going to start with your feet."

When Eric loosens the coils around my ankles, I immediately feel the slack in the twine around my arms and I wiggle my wrists free. He bends down, pulls off my sandal, and dips the towel in the liquid but then he hesitates and looks up at me, "Why are we doing this?" he asks. "You wouldn't let me do it before."

I take a deep breath and lower my voice, "Start with the crack between my toes."

When Eric bends over to apply the paint to my foot, I reach over and pick up the heavy clay pot from the table next to me. With all of my strength, I smash it across the back of Eric's head and he slumps to the floor. I stare at him for a minute, then take the twine that he had used to tie me, pull his arms behind his back, and tie them.

I'm up and I'm running across the room when I hear the front door open and then close, and the sound of a heavy bag dropping to the floor. Wendy walks into the foyer and begins walking up the stairs, "Where's Eric?'

"Bathroom," I tell her.

"Why are you untied?" In her right hands, Wendy is carrying one of those big red clubs that lock up car steering wheels. As she comes up the stairs, she whacks the metal bar several times across the palm of her free hand. I guess she plans to beat me up a bit before leaving me for the Mexican police.

But... I've spent enough time with Sly and Arnold to know the Code of the Warrior. And I know what Margaret White, P.I. would do, and I know what Marga, Amazon Detective would do right now.

So when Wendy nears the top of the stairs, in fact just as her foot touches the top tread, my well muscled right arm rises, and I deliver a really powerful punch to the dead center of her face. Wendy staggers backward, her hand reaching up to her face. "My nose," she gasps and a trickle of blood slides down across her lips.

Without missing a beat, I deliver another right to her face and she falls backwards and then head over heels to the bottom of the stairs. I rush down to the crumpled heap of her, pull her scarf from her purse and use it to tie her wrists. Then I return to her purse, locate the car keys and head for the door.

But the sound of footsteps on the front landing of the house stops me. Is somebody else in on this? Or have the police arrived?

I back up the stairs, slowly, trying to remember if I saw another way out of here. Someone starts pounding on the front door. I look around the large main room. Not knowing which way to go, I open the glass doors and step out onto the balcony, thinking I might be able to drop down off of it and escape. I look down.

Jesus, what a drop! From the balcony, there is a descent of at least sixty feet down past a sheer rock escarpment to the sea. If I jump well and miss the rocks, I still don't think I could survive the fall without a couple of broken bones, maybe a broken back.

As the pounding on the front door grows louder, I glance from one end of the balcony to the other, looking for a stairway, but there's just the narrow balcony and the wooden railing. I can hear noises from the living room now and they're actually in the house. A man's voice calls out, "Hola ... hola?"

The surf is crashing on the rocks below when I look up at the dark tiled roof and see my one last chance. It's a long shot that I can get up on the roof. But if I stand up on the railing of the balcony, and throw myself toward the roof, I just might make it.

I climb up on top of the narrow wooden railing without thinking about the fact that I'm wearing just one sandal and that my other foot is bare which throws off my balance. Reaching down, I try to slip off the one sandal but this action redistributes my weight and that I feel my center of gravity shift. So I stand up quickly, hoping to correct my mistake and I extend both my arms, like a tightrope walker.

But I'm too late and my body has begun to swan dive outward...over the ocean. And even though my feet are still close to the railing, I realize that my arms are too far away to grab hold.

Then the balcony doors burst open, and arms reach out to grab me.

Chapter Twenty-Seven

It's not the Mexican police, it's not Sly, or Arnold, but Dash who grabs me and pulls me up onto the balcony. And I am speechless for several minutes. Finally I manage, "Let's get out of here." We hurry through the living room, although Dash does insist on taking the time to kick Eric in the groin, and then we're out of there. We're in Dash's car, we're on Route # 1 and we're heading North.

I don't even think about Eric and Wendy until we're safely across the border. And even then I'm not thinking straight. Logical thinking requires takes several days, well maybe longer because the first week I'm back in California is full of interviews with newspaper and television reporters. McTeague is delighted but I'm tired and I'd like to get back to my regular life. There's a lot my brain needs to process - the kidnapping, my moment of falling, and of course Dash. I'm enormously grateful to him of course but when I'm near him I'm paralyzed with this powerful feeling of ... discomfort - extreme discomfort.

No matter what I try to do to get rid of this feeling, I can't seem to let down and relax in Dash's presence. And I wonder if maybe I don't want to feel emotionally obligated to him, maybe that's it.

Finally, by the end of the very busy week, I do manage to actually have an almost normal day and I begin to write -that is I actually put words down on paper - sentences, paragraphs, even entire pages, and I realize that my block is broken.

Although I have no idea why. Maybe it was the adrenaline rush of the kidnapping. Or maybe trapped in that limo with so much time to think, I started to see my life and my relationships in a more realistic perspective.

For instance I now understand that my relationship with Sly and Arnold, while friendly and fun, is basically a business collaboration and this realization is liberating. It frees me to write what I want rather than worry about what Sly and Arnold want.

So unencumbered, unblocked, with the energy of a race horse who's been relaxing in the meadow, I begin work. Not just for days, but for weeks, I don't even come out of my studio. So long am I holed up in there, that the staff becomes expert at preparing flat food - that is food that can be slipped under the door. During this period of time, I see no one. I speak to no one. So hard do I work and so long am I in this state of voluntary solitary confinement that I begin to lose all sense of my anchors; my friends, my kids. I even begin to loose my sense of self. There is only the work - the work is everything.

When I finally emerge with the finished product, I'm enormously tired but satisfied. For days I walk around brimming with a wonderful satisfication but then eventually I grow lonely for people.

Yet the usually bustling Casa Stallone is strangely quiet. Sly and Arnold have been off to New York to take a few of their companies public. The boys are at camp all the time. Dash if around of course but I've avoided him and I wonder if I'm in danger of falling into a post-manuscript depression.

So while I wait for my book to appear in stores (The deal McTeague made for me contained the fastest print and distribution clause in book market history,) I take great pains with the details of planning the big book party that Sly promised me.

What I want to do is turn Sly's mansion into a replica of a modern, real life, Lapland Igloo. Because in Lapland, there is a hotel which the Laplanders must not think is cold enough because every winter, next to the hotel, they build an igloo: a big upscale igloo complete with walls and floors of ice and carved beds of ice. In order to cozy up the ice beds, they throw reindeer skins over the tops. There is even a barroom fashioned completely from ice (Caution: Do not lean on the bar since your body heat will melt it). I make up a lot of stuff, but this is true.

I used to joke to Dash's hockey friends that for spring vacation they should take their wives to the Igloo of the Lapland Hotel. But they never got the joke, mostly because they're jocks and stay strictly focused on topics such as whether to shoot high or low on a particular goalie or whether the defense should pinch in past the blue line.

Unfortunately the decorator told me that it would be impossible to convert Sly's mansion into an igloo. So I've had to settle for removing all the furniture and installing plastic ice throughout the entire main floor. Complementing the faux ice floor, which is completely skateable, are decorations celebrating our theme, 'Ancient Rome on Ice.' The pool area has been renovated as the Roman Baths, accurate except for the giant plastic slide into the pool, an Olympic/Disney kind of thing which the decorator suggested.

Initially McTeague came up with the concept of 'Ancient Rome on Ice' to attract lots of press coverage, but now after my abduction, that's no longer necessary. The publicity from my kidnapping has been so massive that the effects are even spilling over to the film project. McTeague is delighted and behaves as if he's planned the whole thing.

I get ready for the party in the large upstairs dressing room of the main house. It has been, in keeping with our theme, decorated to look like an ice hockey locker room of Ancient Rome. Wineskins, sandals, and togas hang from the walls along with face masks, stick tape, and shin pads. This may sound historically incorrect but the discovery of the first ice skates dates their existence back to 60 B.C. so we are still technically accurate.

Guests are encouraged to dress according to time period but really anything goes. My dressing takes no time at all. It's the man's white tee and the black jeans and the fingers through the hair for me. Lips wearing tight black leather looks like a cross between a roller derby queen and a Colosseum gladiator. When she turns around I see that she has managed through careful arrangement of cut-outs in the leather to display her tasteful buttocks tattoo, "Do it!" Hey, why have body art if you can't show it off, right? On her lovely feet she wears black Bauer 5000 hockey skates which will probably be the skate of choice tonight among the studio execs, the development people, and the top agents.

Barb, who will be accompanied by her husband Mitchell for a change, is still dithering about her clothing choice. I can hear her talking to herself while staring into the closet. "Black," she says. "Black is always appropriate." She'll probably match it up with some nice safe pearls.

Although I used to take my cues from Barb, I have to disagree here. This party is not a place to dress safe. In fact life is not a place to dress safe. I watch Lips and Barb drift downstairs. I plan to make a late entrance so I sit around for a while reading <u>Publisher's Weekly</u> and <u>Variety</u>, and assorted other publications checking out the articles about my book/movie project and of course my abduction which has made me the latest victim du jour.

And because of all the personal interest in me, McTeague has planted articles portraying me as so blisteringly brilliant, so curiously creative, so rigidly realistic and yet so innovative that as I read these things, I begin to wonder if I should have my eggs frozen for possible later collaboration with the sperm of Mailer, Vonnegut, or Gaddis. I guess I should go and find McTeague, slap him on the back and tell him what a great job he's done, but I'm a little edgy. I cannot completely forget that ancient Chinese curse: "May all your dreams come true."

I look out the window at the gardens of Sly's estate. The English garden is in full bloom, and through the open window I can smell the orchids below. Farther away in the Italian vineyard, the Tuscany grapevines are growing, and the olive trees from Crete are flourishing. It's summer...full and ripe. And it's difficult to believe that I've been here for so long.

I gaze out Sylvester's window for a while thinking about what a long road I've traveled and how I should be enjoying my success more. After all, my effort, while creative, has had about it the feel of a great military campaign. And even though I'm a woman, I have always felt a spiritual closeness to the great warrior heroes of the past, Alexander the Great, Ghengis Khan, and Napoleon being my special favorite because he said "Imagination rules the World." And isn't this the warrior's feast? Isn't this where my buddies and I get to celebrate by playing with the scalps of the vanquished, eating the brains of the enemy, and stuff like that.

I wait until the joint is really jumping before beginning my grand descent down the big staircase. I am trying for Lillian Hellman sophistication, but my stride is not too smooth considering that I am walking in my Bauer 5000 hockey skates. I step off the bottom step of the plastic-treaded stairs, glide onto the plastic ice, grab a complimentary toga, skate around, and survey the place.

Tony Lamboni is serving from a long bar in the corner of one of the large front rooms. McTeague was really against this, but he had to give in because Sylvester and I insisted on it.

Arnold and Sylvester aren't here yet, although they will be arriving later by private jet.

One of the first things I notice is how strangely everyone is moving. Master Wong wearing a wine red leotard is gliding from room to room in his various T'ai Chi poses, the picture of serenity. But the rest of the crowd looks herky-jerky. I guess it's because those who can skate, do, and those who can't, have opted for shuffling around in slippers, which does make for an odd-looking party. Elliott Stanton is one of the shufflers. He comes by to shake my hand. "I hear the first printing set a new record." I nod like it's nothing but really it is - like a dream.

A little group forms around me: Norman Mailer, Tom Wolfe, Bret Ellis, Hunter Thompson, Jay MacInerny, William Burroughs. They are slavish with their praise, even the minimalists. So I give them a little time before excusing myself to go check on my friends. Mary Pat and Gita are over in a corner arguing over whether there is a place for religion in the world of psychiatry.

But then there is a commotion at the front door, which draws quite a crowd. It is the arrival of the actress Laura Lee Koharski, who has been chosen to play Marga in the film. She is astride her Arabian stallion which is extremely problematic because there have already been allegations from animal rights groups about what she has been doing with the horse. Laura wants to get the stallion, Jewels, inside the house to join the party. I don't really think he can skate, but figure what the hell. After conferring with Candy and Mary Pat I tell Snake to find something soft to slip over the horse's hooves. Snake hasn't dressed Roman. He's wearing his usual leather vest and scraggly jeans, and I'm glad because Snake is an original and should never conform to convention. Joining me at Snake's silver canape tray are McTeague dressed in an elegant combination of Armani, Baldessarini, and Bauer skates, accompanied by Ivan the Russian hairstylist who is wearing a pre-glasnost suit and antique skates. But McTeague is rather a nervous mess due to the fact that he's working, so I slip away from him.

The last to arrive, and the most quiet are the relatives. When Dash comes in with the boys, I notice that their hair is neatly trimmed, and still wet from the shower, and they are dressed in sport coats, shirts, and ties. I also notice that my sons, who are precision skaters, slip along the ice instead in soft-soled shoes. This strikes me as disingenuous but I figure it's just another of Dash's misguided attempts to influence me.

When Dash brings them up to me. I can tell from the look on their faces that they are under strict instructions about how to behave. Each one shakes hands with me; Dash Jr, Bobby, Wayne, and Dart. Each son says a variation of the same thing. "Congratulations, Mom. We're really proud of you." Then they stand behind Dash until he tells them that they can go and eat.

Dash also compliments me, "You did great, Molly. This is amazing." It's a nice compliment, and I should be savoring this moment, when my foot is figuratively on his neck. After all he was the one who disdained the literary production of my laundry room back when we lived together in the land of snow and ice.

But I find I'm not enjoying my superior position. I'm kind of detached, although I do notice that Dash looks uncomfortable and that his eyes are a little dead. Like a jerk I bring this up, along with some semi-nasty implication that maybe he isn't really so happy with my success, which I can't believe I'm saying because ever since he came to California, he has never said or implied that in any way. And he did really save my life by getting me out of Mexico.

But Dash takes no offense. "I'm glad you've made it, Molly. It's just that," and he motions toward the party, "this isn't me."

"I know, you're Miller Beer and the Rangers game."

"Okay...I think you've proven whatever you needed to prove." Then he clears his throat like he's going to say something significant, something difficult. "And I've been making some changes, which has been a pain in the ass for me, but that's okay because every now and then a man's got to do something he doesn't want to do." He looks at me for my reaction, but I don't know what to say to this.

"Anyway the point is, I've been hoping you would notice. I've been waiting for a while now, and I guess I don't really know how much more wait I've got left in me."

He looks sincere and I think I should be touched, but all I can think is - Nice touch, Dashermeister. Ruin my big evening why don't you? I don't say this, though. I just take off in my skates and accidentally hip check him as I go by, so he spills his drink all over the plastic ice.

Arnold and Sylvester arrive later in the evening, as they promised. This roughly coincides with the change in the weather. All kinds of strange weather predictions have been made, like a hurricane of tropical proportions, which never happens in Southern California and another scientist from Cal Tech has claimed that a big Tsunami is approaching. The Tsunami, the giant wave that comes up every thirty to fifty years, empties harbors, and generally demolishes the shoreline with a fifty-foot-high wall of water, usually only hits around Japan, and everyone in L.A. is griping that the weather is just another form of Japanese takeover. Like everyone else I've become mentally accustomed to fires, mudslides, and earthquakes but a hurricane and a big Tsunami?

Arnold and Sylvester look jet lagged, which is to be expected for a couple of moguls who've been toiling in the fields of franchises and endorsements. But what I didn't expect was that they would look pained and horrified as well. Sylvester speaks quickly, "Molly, we were on the way back home in the Lear before we had a chance to read the final copy of your book and we believe there are some ... major problems." Arnold composes his face into an icy block, as Sly continues, "For one thing, we knew that your story included a romantic subplot..."

"That's right."

"But according to what we just read - Marga...uh...romances my character Marcus Aurelius and then two years later she...uh...romances Arnold's character, Catullus Brutus."

I think about everything Sly and Arnold have taught me - like how you must take every opportunity to increase the action, sometimes even piggy backing one action with another. I guess I'm trying to gauge the exact nature of their objection. "Oh, so you think the two romances should take place simultaneously?" I ask. "What a great idea! That would demonstrate Marga's fierce independence and total freedom so - so graphically."

Sylvester looks down at his shoes. "Well, we were thinking that maybe Marga could use her total freedom to choose monogomy."

"That's a very patriarichal concept."

"But Molly we live in a patriarchial culture," Sly points out.

"You have to look at the big picture," I tell them. "Macho is on the way out. It's time to adapt to something new. Don't you see what a great opportunity this is to show the world that you're bigger than conventional trends?"

"Look Molly we're not going to play your heroine's....boy toys." Sylvester's face is getting red and he really looks ...well mad. Arnold is massaging his temples.

Okay...having spent most of my adult life living with five males, I ought to recognize the tone of injured male pride. And the last thing I want to do is hurt Sly or Arnold, so I try to say something conciliatory but all I can sputter is "Well...Well..." because what I'm really thinking is that this is my story, right?

"You'll have to make changes," Sly says while Arnold nods emphatically."

"But it's too late to change anything. The book is already published." I make a big helpless hand waving gesture here.

"Now wait a minute, Sly." Arnold interrupts in the problem solving voice, the voice that addresses world hunger and stuff like that. "Lots of times a book has a different ending from the movie. Why can't we let Molly do the book her way and then we'll just make whatever changes are necessary for the movie."

Sylvester takes a deep breath. "I see your point. It's not too late for the film. We'll trim down to one romantic subplot and we'll give the story a really great action ending."

I fold my arms across my chest and compose my body into a statue. "I don't think so, guys. I'm very clear on this." I tell them with an edge of authority in my voice.

Sly and Arnold both turn a sickly pale shade and Sylvester sits down very quietly. I guess this must be like a nightmare to them. So I decide I'd better explain things to them slowly, "It took me quite a while to realize that all along in a totally unconsciously manner, I've been writing a different kind of a story. And it's taken a lot of soul-searching for me to recognize exactly what I've been doing and what is the inevitable result."

Chapter Twenty-Eight

I have to stay up all night talking with them.

They just can't seem to accept the fact that personal freedom needs to be the concluding element. The ending is the most powerful part of the story and a war victory just doesn't do it for me. Love is stronger than war, right? The heart is the most important muscle in the body, right? I suggest to them that maybe it's a girl thing and that as guys they don't need to understand it, but they just frown, arrange their bodies into commanding positions, and try to talk me into rewriting.

At some point I think one of them called a lawyer, probably after I explained to them how by virute of my failure to sign that legal contract they kept leaving in my office, I still own the story - completely. And as the owner, future changes will be made only at my discretion.

They threaten me with pulling out of the movie but I don't believe them, I think they'll come around. Strangely enough, I don't feel very involved in this. I'm completely detached from the violent emotions swirling around me because I know this is right. And when you have that feeling, that in-the-bones certainty, that's when you take your stand.

All night long Sylvester and Arnold argue, and all night long the wind whips up outside. I look out the window and it looks like an exterior shot for the movie <u>Key Largo</u> when they're waiting for the big hurricane to destroy everything.

By dawn there is early activity in the compound, and I know the reason is that an evacuation has been planned for this temporary lull in the storm. I know this because last night the cable network kept interrupting the shopping channel (to which I had resorted as an escape from Sly and Arnold) with emergency weather bulletins.

Personally I don't believe there is a real emergency and find the whole thing amusing, but after the night-long argument, I'm too tired to suggest that in this land of disaster, this land where fire, earthquake, and freeway catastrophes are almost ordinary, why make such a fuss about a little wind and rain?

So I take a solitary position on the front steps between the Neo-Corinthian columns, just to watch what's going on. It's the first time since I've been in L.A. that the sky has been really dark.

Sylvester and Arnold follow me out there, still trying to persuade me, but I negate the impact of their arguments by distracting them with irrelevant esoteric historical objections. This really throws them into a tizzy.

Barb is the first to appear outside the mansion, wearing that red Nancy Reagan suit that she wore the first time she arrived. She has her two huge suitcases and Mitch's one little leather suitcase. Motioning Snake over to her, she begins the orders. "Put our things in the car. We're going to the airport."

Hearing this, Sylvester interrupts his long impassioned argument with me, to tell Barb that the airport is closed. He suggests that she and Mitch evacuate with the rest of the staff and points to a van pulling up carrying Lips, Lucky, Nick, Trip, Vinnie and assorted mansion personnel.

Barb raises her eyebrows. "I don't think so. What about you? We'll go with you."

"No can do, Barbie. Snake is taking me and Arnold up to see Clint. Molly, you're coming along."

I shake my head in the negative.

"We insist," Sylvester says.

I start to smirk. What's he going to do? Pick me up and put me in the car? When it occurs to me that those may be his exact plans, I stop smirking.

Hearing the sound of the Humvee, I turn to see Betsy getting out of the vehicle. She walks over to Sylvester, wraps herself around him and says, "I forgot to pick up the fruit and imported water."

"That's okay," he says. "At least you got yourself here."

"I'm not taking a car trip with her," I tell Sly.

Sylvester gives me the heavy-lidded gaze. "I've been meaning to talk to you about Betsy. We're planning this project..."

His voice drifts off. I only hear pieces of the rest of the explanation, something about a collaboration between Cal Tech and M.I.T. and Arnold's people to do some kind of film about environmental heroism. I hear words like realism and hope for the future and Chernobyl, so I know it's a load of bull.

I also know what he's up to. It's not that I think I own him or anything. Naturally Sylvester can pursue whatever relationships he chooses. But to bring that woman along on a trip with Arnold and me, to add a stranger to the Three Musketeers is, I feel, an act of disloyalty.

Dash and the boys appear from behind the main house. They carry duffel bags, which they throw into Victor and I have this momentary ridiculous B.C. retro thought that I should be going with them. Instead I walk over and kiss the boys goodbye. They look so young and strong. They smell of soap from their early morning showers.

Mitchell pulls up in a rented red convertible, that he didn't have last night. "Get in," he tells Barb, and for once she does what he says.

"I straightened out the crew for you." Mitch tells Dash. "Did you know they were taking home lumber?"

Dash looks amused, "Thanks, Mitch." Mitch waves and drives off. He has pulled out of the driveway and Dash is just standing alone when it happens.

Out of nowhere, the dark sky opens up and a bright synapse of lightning streaks down toward earth. The sky directly behind Dash is so intensely bright that it looks like a giant photographic flash, with so much wattage I can only see the black outline of Dash's body. Then the lightning hits the ground and travels.

I don't remember seeing Dash get knocked out, but I know that I have been knocked unconscious. I know this because when I wake up, I'm lying face down in the mulch of a flower bed and my first sensation is smell: the wet musty mulch, the freshly cut grass, the English orchids a few feet away.

I try to move my fingers and then my feet, and they do work. I sit up. Actually I realize my body is moving alot easier than it was before I got knocked out. It's as if my joints have been oiled, or I've had an especially effective chiropractic realignment. I also feel strangely peaceful and relaxed.

I wonder what happened to me. If I was struck by lightning then wouldn't I be dead? Maybe it was a traveling ball of lightning. Maybe I was just close enough to be knocked out but not close enough to be killed.

I walk over to where Dash is lying face down on the grass. The boys are unhurt. They're clustered around Dash in shocked disbelief. By now I know I'm okay, but I'm thinking frantically, Oh no, Dash can't be dead. He can't be dead. I'll just give him mouth to mouth. But I don't know mouth to mouth resuscitation. I wonder if I can approximate mouth to mouth with some sort of satisfactory result? I know I have to try. But before I can even bend down to him, Dash starts flopping his legs around, and then he opens his eyes and sits up.

We all laugh with nervous relief and help Dash keep his balance as he gets up to a shaky standing position. As he raises himself I'm struck by the fact that all around his body is just a little bit of light. As if he's still glowing from the lightning. I know that's impossible. So maybe it's just an image my retina has retained from the original event.

I don't know. I don't care, I'm just glad he's alive. I throw my arms around him and press my face into his neck. That's when I notice how good he smells. Maybe it's just soap and cologne, but wow, he smells great! I take a step back to look him over carefully. Now Dash has always been an attractive man, but after you've been married awhile you tend to forget about things like that. And eighteen years have gone by. Still I am surprised at how good he looks. I mean let's fact it, Dash is a hunk. How long has it been since I realized that fact? I can't remember. And I can't remember Dash looking so good to me since well...since the beginning.

I take another long look at him. As I study his straight features and wide gray eyes, the wind lifts a fringe of the dark reddish gold hair that falls across his forehead and it does occur to me at this moment, that I am noticing the subtle shading nuances of his hair. Dash gives me a look. What is it about him that just does it for me? Why does he make me feel lightheaded? And why do I like it?

The little hairs on the back of my neck go up. Ever so slightly, completely unconsciously, and independent of the rest of my bodily functions, my heart increases its beat.

Then I remember that the only area in which Dash has never ever disappointed me, was in the bedroom. He must be thinking the same thing because oblivious to everyone else, we both begin walking in the direction of the house.

The boys don't even notice us. They have begun playing street hockey with wadded-up balls of paper and tape. But Sylvester must have figured things out because he herds them into his car and calls after us. "I'll take care of the gang. There's a storm cellar in the basement. Fully equipped... wine, stereo, king-sized bed."

I look back at Sylvester and Arnold. They look far away and kind of small. I notice that both of them have perfectly styled brown hair. I notice that they look over-groomed and over-dressed. Don't get me wrong, I love them like brothers and we'll always be friends, but isn't gold jewelry and black silk Versace a bit much? And isn't Arnold's enormous Winston Churchill cigar just a bit affected? I also notice that no matter what the fan magazines say, neither one of these action heroes is over six feet two inches tall, while my own husband is a certifiable six feet, three.

Dash's arm is on my back, and that slight pressure combined with my intense awareness of his physical presence is all-encompassing to me, so I continue to walk toward the house.

As I wave goodbye to Arnold and Sly, I continue to notice little things about Dash, like the fact that his hair is plain, not styled, and that this past year, he's gotten just a little gray around the temples. He doesn't wear any jewelry at all, never wears black. And as I look from Stallone to Schwarzenegger to Dash, I cannot help but notice that not only in terms of height and style but also in terms of sweetness and strength -- my husband is bigger than both of them.

Epilogue

I'm in Idaho now. Montana was too crowded. Yep, I'm living in the land of Hemingway.

Dash and I and the boys have a nice little place near Big Sky with our very own ice rink in the backyard and our own Zamboni. Well, actually it's two places. Although we co-own the property, we each have our own house. Dash wasn't too crazy about this, but it wasn't up to him. The way I see it, is this - Yes, I do believe he is the greatest pair of pants that ever walked the face of the earth, but this doesn't change the fact that he is on probation. And even if he wasn't, I have adopted a new philosophy regarding men. I take it from the wisdom of Charles Dickens, "Make them laugh, make them cry, make them wait."

Next to my house, Dash has built me a writing studio. I'm working on a new epic historical now. The only problem I've been having is the telephone. They're all over me - the boys from Hollywood. They want me to consult on all their projects. Something about weaving the romantic subplot in as a more integral part of the story. But it's all about money. It's money calling...always.

The big action films aren't grossing like they used to. Audiences are yearning for the old virtues. The magazines are filled with articles about the death of the old-style action hero who functions in a pared-down minimalist world and the emergence of character stories, historical settings, and romance.

Sylvester and Arnold won't leave me alone. They're in this humongous fight about where I'm going to buy my ski house. Will it be Telluride or Aspen? I keep telling them, "Boys, don't fight or I'll buy property in the

Caribbean" and that shuts them up for a little while -- until they get back to trying to discover the plot of my new epic. They both want in, even though all they know about the project is that it's a big historical saga.

The development people think my story is impossible to film, politically incorrect, and wildly improbably. They think it has too much romance and too many characters, and the story is way too long. But they want me to write it anyway. I'm the only one they'll allow on it. I guess it's because I'm living proof.

Lightning <u>can</u> strike twice.

About the Author

I was born in Elizabeth, New Jersey on October 31, 1947 – Halloween.

I went to Syracuse University to study law, become a lawyer when there were very few women practicing law. I was successful and had photographic memory, which helped immensely. The book is a figment of my imagination written in between court cases when I become bored.